T0198843

# Teenage Romance

♥ ♥

*Fiction*
*A Collection of Short Stories*

*By*

♥ *K. M. Marsh* ♥

iUniverse, Inc.
New York   Bloomington

Teenage Romance
A Collection of Short Stories

iUniverse books may be ordered through booksellers or by contacting:

iUniverse
1663 Liberty Drive
Bloomington, IN 47403
www.iuniverse.com
1-800-Authors (1-800-288-4677)

Because of the dynamic nature of the Internet, any Web addresses or links contained in this
book may have changed since publication and may no longer be valid. The views expressed
in this work are solely those of the author and do not necessarily reflect the views of the
publisher, and the publisher hereby disclaims any responsibility for them.

ISBN: 978-1-4401-8360-7 (sc)
ISBN: 978-1-4401-8361-4 (ebook)

Printed in the United States of America

iUniverse rev. date:12/03/2009

Dedicated to all my friends and family
who kept encouraging me when
I wanted to give up and quit.

A special thank you goes to
my daughter Laura
who without her continued
encouragement
this book might never
have been published.

Thank you one and all!

Sincerely, K. M. Marsh

# Teenage Romance

## Table of Contents

# One
## The Mysterious Voice

Lynetta and Jack were part of a group of young people involved in their local theater. They enjoyed putting on productions for their friends and family and the local towns-people. They had just put in a full day of rehearsing a new show. They were both happy but so tired. Lynetta said to Jack, "I'm going home to a nice relaxing , hot bath!" Jack replied, "I think I'll take a quick shower and a short nap. I'll call you later after I get a little rest, see you later Lynetta, I love you." "Okay! I'll be waiting, I love you too! Bye Jack."

While Lynetta was in the tub all she could think about was Jack. Thinking of him made her smile. Soon she was finished with her bath and dressed again.

Meanwhile in Jack's apartment he couldn't fall asleep because he kept seeing her face in his mind. Going over every detail, the way her eyes sparkle and dance each time she smiles. Her skin so soft to the touch that he can't help but caress it so tenderly. Jack gave up on trying to sleep so he called Lyn. Her phone rang and she answered, "Hello?" "Hi Baby. Miss me?" "Of course I did!" "Wanna see a movie tonight, or shall we do something else?" " We could take a walk in the moonlight under the stars." "Oh I like how you think. ( he smiled really big). I haven't eaten yet have you?" "No and I'm a little hungry." "That settles it. I'll take you to dinner and then we can go for a walk afterward, what do you think?" " I like the sound of that." "Alright. I'll pick you up in an hour. Is that enough time for you?" "Sure, I'll be waiting." (she smiled sweetly). They both hung up.

A few minutes passed and Lynetta's phone rang, she answered it "Hello?" A strangers voice said " Hi. What are you doin' tonight?" Lynetta, (not recognizing the voice) said, "Who is this please?" The voice said "I'm a very devoted fan of yours who really wishes you'd dump Jack and go out with me." She said, "I can't do that, goodbye" and she hung up. She got a tight feeling in her throat after the call. A couple of minutes passed and her phone rang again. She jumped with fear and random thoughts passed through her mind. (Should I answer it? Maybe it's Jack or Alyssa), it rang again and she still didn't answer. She thought- "If it's Jack he'll wonder why I'm not answering." The phone rang a third time. She answered guardedly, "Hello?"

"There you are. I was beginning to worry. What took so long to pick up the phone?" She thought to herself, (Whew it's Jack, what a relief). "Oh, I-I mislaid my phone. What did you want?" " I meant to ask you, before I hung up, do you have a special place where you would like to eat?" "No, not really, any place with you is special!" "Oh Lyn you're so sweet, it's no wonder I love you sooo much! See you soon." Then they hung up. "I'd better get ready. Jack will be here soon." She put on Jack's favorite outfit, (a powder blue velvety soft pant with matching jacket). Her little sister walked by Lyn's room and peeked in, "OO Jack must be coming over, cause that's his favorite outfit of yours." (They both smiled and Lynetta nodded to Stella). "Yes, he is Stella. He's taking me to dinner and no you can't go. BUT, if you're a good girl for mom maybe we'll bring you back some ice cream or something." "Oh, alright." Stella said, a little disappointed. "Hey L- who was it that called a minute ago, Jackky?" Lynetta froze for a moment.

Then she said, sharply, "Uh, just a wrong number." She couldn't get the callers voice out of her head. She thought it had sounded vaguely familiar but couldn't think who it might be. There was a knock on the door. Lynetta opened the door. It's Jack. "Whoa, did you put that on just for me? You know it's my favorite?!" "Well, yes, I did." (she said slightly blushing). "I like it, I like it a lot." He had a huge smile on his face. "Are you ready?" "I just have to tell my mom we're leaving."

"Mom, Jack's here, we're going to dinner now. See you later."

Her Mom came into the room, "Okay have a good time and don't stay out too late, you need your rest for tomorrow." Jack said, "I'll have her home by 10:00 or 10:30 at the latest, goodbye Mrs H." "Alright thank you Jack. Have a good time you two!"

Jack and Lynetta went to his car. Jack said "Wait a minute, stand right there."(he reached into the car for something) "I've got something for you." (She looked curiously at him.) "What? I thought we were just going to dinner?" "We are but first..." Just then he pulled a red rose from behind his back and gave it to her with a kiss. "You didn't have to do that." "Yes, I did. A beautiful girl should be given roses whenever possible and a red rose stands for love, so this rose is a symbol of my love for you." "Oh Jack it's beautiful. Thank you." They shared a very passionate kiss. Then he opened the car door for her and closed it after her. He got in and off they went to dinner. After dinner he said, "What do you say we go get some ice cream for dessert and we can take some home for Stella and your mom?" "That's a great idea!" At his car Jack opened her door, helped her in and closed it after her. (Wow, what a gentleman.)

Just as Jack went around the car to his door her phone rang. She let out a gasp and was suddenly frightened. She thought, (What if it's him again? What 'll I do? If I don't answer it Jack will wonder why and if I do and it is him... I can't tell Jack, he'll worry too much... , she answered quietly, "Hello?" (Male voice)- "Hi baby, How are you?" "Will you please stop calling me?" Voice- "Don't worry, your boyfriend can't hear me and you haven't told him about me, so it's cool."

"Maybe I have told him about you?" Voice- "You haven't told him because you're afraid of how he'll react, he might dump you. So have you figured out who I am yet?" "No and I'm sure I don't want to. Now leave me alone. PLEASE!"

She hung up just as Jack opened his door and just as she put her phone away Jack got in the car. "Did I just hear your phone ring?" She tried not to look surprised when she answered. "Oh, yeah, it was just a wrong number." Then, in her best 'operators' voice (fingers squeezing her nose), "I'm sorry, you have reached a disconnected number, please check the number and try your call later."

"Hey, that's pretty good. If your acting career doesn't work out you could become a phone operator." "VERY Funny Jack. Ha! Ha!"

At the ice cream place they shared each others ice cream. It was getting late so they got some ice cream for Lyn's mom and little sis Stella. Back at Lynetta's house Jack walked her to her door. Lynetta asked "Would you like to come in for a little while?" He said "Okay, but only long enough to say goodnight then I need to go home." "Okay. It has been a long day hasn't it? (sigh) I miss you already!"

Jack looked at her and said, "Come here you...(Jack took her in his arms and kissed her passionately then he whispered), I wish I could be your pillow tonight. I just want to hold you close all night."

Lynetta thought to herself, "Did he hear me on the phone in the car?" She opened the door and they went in. Her mom was sitting in the chair, reading and looked up as they came in. "Hello. Did you have a good time?" "Hi. Mrs. H. yes, we sure did and here she is all safe and sound and by 10:00 as I promised." "Thank you Jack. I can always count on you." "Oh, here, we brought back some ice cream for you and Stella." (Stella came bouncing in as always.) "ALRIGHT! Thanks a lot! Jack you are so awesome!" "Thank you Jack. That was very thoughtful. Well I think I'll go to my room, goodnight kids."

After mom left the room Stella blurted out "Hey Netta, did you get any more wrong numbers on your phone tonight?" Lyn just glared at Stella. Jack said, "What?" Just then Lynetta's phone rang again and Jack saw the look of fear on her face. "Hey baby, I'm here. Has someone been calling and harassing you?" She didn't quite know what she should say to that. "Lynetta, answer me and I want the truth!" (Was he getting angry or just very worried?) Suddenly her phone stopped ringing.

Jack said "I'm not leaving here until we talk about this, even if it takes all night." Lynetta started to tell Jack what happened but then she began to cry. Jack reached out and wrapped his arms around her. He said "It will be alright. I'm not angry just concerned." He brushed a tear from her cheek then softly kissed her there. "Please tell me. I want to help." Lynetta pulled away. "I...I can't. Just go home Jack." "Why? Why won't you tell me?" (He paused a few moments then sadly asked:) "Is there...someone else?" She looked at him and couldn't believe what she was hearing. She looked again and saw a tear in his eye. "Oh Jack, NO! You're the only man for me. How can you ask or even think that? I Love YOU!" "But you won't tell me what's going on. I can't stand seeing you this upset. Please tell me!"

So she took a deep breath and began again. "Remember this

afternoon, when I came home to have my bath?" "Sure, I remember." "Well, a few minutes after you called me, my phone rang, I answered it thinking it was you again but instead it was a guy claiming to be a fan. He said he wanted me to dump you for him. I told him I can't do that and now he keeps calling me. I was afraid, that if you found out some guy was calling me, you would think I was...cheating on you and I'd lose you, not just as a boyfriend, but as a friend. I couldn't bear that."

"Wow, that's a heavy load for you to carry." "I'm sorry Jack. I wouldn't blame you if you wanted to leave me. I can see how this must look to you." She turned away and began to cry again. He took her chin in his hand and gently turned her face toward his and said, "Hey, I love you. And in my book that means a lot. Honey, I trust you. Do you still love me?"

"More than anything." "Then we can get through this and anything else that comes along, right?" "I love you so much Jack." "I love you too baby, come here." Jack took her hand and lead her to the couch, as they sat there he put his arms around her and held her close. As she laid her head on his chest she felt a huge sense of relief. Jack gently caressed her hair. Not realizing that he was speaking out loud Jack softly said, "How did I ever get so lucky to find someone as wonderful as you are?" Lynetta turned her face toward his, smiled and said, "I'm the lucky one." "Then their lips touched in a romantic and passionate kiss but, they were interrupted when her phone started to ring. Lynetta looked frightened. Jack said, firmly, "Go ahead and answer it then let me listen."

"Hello?" Voice on the phone: "Hi Baby, how ya doin' tonight? I'll bet old Jack has hit the road, now that he knows about us." (Lynetta was holding the phone between Jack and her so Jack could hear everything the caller said.) Suddenly    Jack took the phone from Lynetta and said, "Well you're wrong there. Now forget this phone number and leave my girl alone. I'm not leaving her so stop calling her. She's mine. If you call her again you'll be dealing with the police. Goodbye." Jack hung the phone up and gave it back to Lynetta. "I don't think he'll be calling you back again. I think I made it quite clear that you are *not* available. Can you go to sleep now? Remember rehearsal is bright and early at 6 a. m. tomorrow  morning."

While looking at Lynetta, Jack started thinking, (I wish you could sleep in my arms tonight, then I would know that you're safe. But at least you're with your mom now and that guy knows now that I'm not going anywhere. So if he's smart he won't *ever* call back.) Then he said out loud, "I love you Lynetta. Remember, there isn't anything so terrible that you can't tell me. We're a team and we can handle <u>anything</u> as long as we do it together, right?"

"Right! I love you too babe...and Jack?" "Yeah?" "Thanks for being so wonderful and understanding." "You're welcome sweetheart, have sweet dreams." Then Jack kissed her goodnight and went home.

# Two

# A New Boyfriend for Lynetta?

The radio came on: "Wake up all you sleepy heads. It's 5 a. m. Time to get up, grab that wakeup juice and start your day..." Jack got up and headed for the shower. After he got dressed he looked over at his headboard and saw Lynetta's picture. He smiled and went over to it, picked it up and kissed it, "Good morning sweetheart, I sure do miss you."

At Lynetta's house her mom was fixing breakfast for Lynetta and her little sister Stella. Lynetta got up, showered and dressed. When Lynetta came into the kitchen, her mom turned around and said, "Good morning honey." "Good morning mom, shall I set the table?" "Yes, that will be great." Stella came bouncing in, "Hi Netta, can I help?" "Sure squirt. You want to set plates or forks?" Stella said, "You can set the plates, they're still too heavy for me." "Okay," she said with a smile. Mom said, "Alright breakfast is almost ready, who's hungry?" The girls said in unison- "ME!" Then Lynetta said, "Mom, may I call Jack and invite him over for breakfast? The last time I looked in his kitchen, well let me just say, he really is truly a bachelor. I don't think he really has <u>anything</u> for breakfast." "Really? Oh that <u>is</u> sad. Well, we have plenty so, go ahead, call him up and invite him." "Thanks Mom."Back at Jack's place- Jack went to the kitchen, opened the fridge "NOTHING", opened the cupboard, "NOTHING, my cupboards are so bare even the mice have to go out to eat." (The phone rang, Jack answered), "Yo, talk to me."

"Good morning sweetheart." "It is now. I really do miss you." "Jack, have you had breakfast yet?" "No, and it looks like I'll have to go out to get anything. My cupboards are so bare it looks like I just moved in."

"Why don't you come over here? My mom's fixing breakfast and she said we have plenty. She also said I could call to invite you to breakfast." "I don't want to intrude on your family time." "You're not, I'm inviting you. Besides you just said you'd have to go out for breakfast so there's no reason you can't come over here." "Well I can't argue that one." "So, you'll come over?" "Sure, how can I resist such a charming hostess as yourself? See you soon."

Minutes later Jack arrived at Lynetta's home. (Knock Knock), Stella yelled out, "I'll get it." She opened the door, "Hi Jack." "Hi Stella. What's for breakfast?" "Come and see." Jack could already smell the wonderful aroma coming from the kitchen.

"OO  pancakes, they smell terrific." Mrs H. was at the stove cooking stacks of pancakes. " Good morning Jack, I'm glad you could join us this morning. I didn't think you would turn down the chance to have a good home cooked breakfast. Go ahead and sit down. Breakfast is ready."

Soon everyone was eating Mrs. H's delicious pancakes smothered in butter and syrup. "Here Jack, there's plenty. Have some more." "No thank you! I'm full. But that was awesome. Thank you for inviting me!" "You're quite welcome Jack."

"Well Lynetta, we'd better go if we're going to make rehearsal on time." "Oh, rehearsal, you're right! We'd better go." "Since I'm already here do you want to ride with me?" "Sure, I don't need my car today." "Let's go then. Thanks again for that wonderful breakfast, Mrs. H." "You're welcome Jack, come back again We love to have you." Jack and Lynetta got into Jack's car and headed for the studio.

Jack's phone rang, he answered it, "Yo, talk to me." "Hey dude, where are you?" "Hey Leon, I'm headed for the studio, I went to Lyn's house for breakfast. Her mom made pancakes and man they were sooo good! I had so many I'm not sure I can dance now!"

"So is Lynetta with you or is she driving down?" "No, she's right here with me. We should be there soon." "Okay, we'll see you when you get here. Tell Lyn I said Hi. See ya later." "Later dude." "Leon said Hi. He's already at the studio." Jack and Lynetta arrived at the studio with a few minutes to spare.

"Hey look, here come Leon and Adrianne." "Morning guys," said Leon. (Adrianne waved.) Lynetta and Jack said, "Hi everyone." Adrianne said, "Danny's about to start the stretches." Jack said, "So, let's go workout." The director Danny addressed the cast: "Good morning everybody. Did everyone get a good nights sleep? I hope so. Well people, let's get to it." Danny put everyone through a good ½ hour warm up and stretching workout, (to help prevent injuries.)

"Okay, everyone looks great! Let's rest and cool down for five minutes, not ten or fifteen I said five. (Just then Danny got a phone call.) After the call he said, "Jack and Lynetta come over here please?!" Jack asked, "What's up Danny?" "I have some new steps for Leon and Adrianne I'd like to run through first. Would you and Lynetta sit the first 15 or 20 minutes out for me please?" "Sure Danny, Whatever you say." "Lynetta?" "Yeah, sure Danny."

Jack said to Lynetta, "Why do I think your mom had something to do with that?" Lynetta just smiled at him and shrugged her shoulders. Alyssa and Brian came over. "Hi! Jack, Hi! Lynetta ." "Hi guys. What's up?" Lyssa to Lynetta, "Do you want to go shopping after rehearsal with Adrianne and me?" "Sure, that sounds like fun but I don't have my car here." "That's alright we can take you home."

Brian said, "So Jack, do you want to go shoot some hoops after rehearsal with me and Leon?" "Sounds cool, let's do it. I need to take Lynetta home first and I can meet you at the court."

Lynetta came over, "Jack, you don't need to take me home I'm going shopping with the girls this afternoon and they'll take me home." "Alright, sounds great!"

Danny came over, (clapping to get everyone's attention) and said, "Okay everybody, let's go! We have a lot of work to do today. Let's get to it. Show me what you've got. If you work extra hard today I may let you go a little early. So let's go!"

Danny and all the cast put in a lot of hard work but everyone enjoyed it. Danny was so pleased with their performance he let them all go one hour early.

"Alright everybody, great job today. I'll give you some time off today cause you all earned it. Have a great time, see you all bright and early tomorrow."

The girls got in Alyssa's car and headed to the mall, after saying goodbye to the guys. Jack said, "Okay guys, let's go do some hoops!" The guys spent a couple of hours shooting hoops. Suddenly Jack said, "Hey, I'm thirsty. Let's go get something cold...at the Mall." Brian said, "Why the Mall?" Leon said to Brian, "Dude, the *girls* are probably at the Mall. Maybe we'll run into them?!" Jack said, "Alright Leon, I like how you think man! Let's go!"

The guys got to the Mall and went in. They were headed for a cold drink stand when Leon looked over and saw a good friend across the way. "Hey Tay Tay, what's up?" "Well, Hi there Leon, how y'all doin' sweetie? Hey little bit, how's your mama?" "She's good, how are you?" "Good, good, y'all is lookin' fine. Say Leon tell your mama I said Hi! And have her give me a call or I'll try to call her, Okay?" "Okay!" "It's so good to see you precious. Now I got to go so give lil Tay Tay a big ole hug now? Hope I see you later!" Leon and Tay Tay waved goodbye to each other.

"Dude WHO is that? She is sooo cool!!" said Jack. "Oh she's been a family friend ever since I can remember." Brian asked, "Is she always like that?" "Yeah, she is." he said with a sly sideways smile.

The girls decided to go get some cold drinks. Shopping is very thirsty work. As they came around a corner Jesse, an old friend of Lyn's, came up behind her, grabbed her and gave her a huge kiss on the lips. Just then Jack, Leon and Brian came around the other corner and Jack couldn't believe what he saw. There, right in front of him, he saw his girl kissing another guy. Jack suddenly slipped back around the corner so she couldn't see him. The others followed. Leon said, "Dude maybe it's not what it looks like." Jack peeked around the corner and then he saw what *appeared* to be *his* girl locked in a rather passionate embrace of that same guy.

Brian said, "Hey, maybe Leon's right. You know Lynetta is <u>so</u> in love with you it <u>has</u> to be something *totally* innocent." "I want to believe that more than anything! But seeing her with another guy, *like that*...I don't even know what to do or even think. Should I confront her? Should I wait to see if she tells me about it? or What? I'm going home guys. I'll see you later." Leon said, "Jack, don't read more into it than it probably is."

Jack shook his head and drove home. He was so upset that he didn't remember how he got there. He thought – "Maybe my friends are right. I'll just call her and get this whole thing straightened out."

He called Lynetta's house, "Hello?" "Hi Mrs. H. This is Jack. Could I talk to Lynetta please?" "Oh, I'm sorry Jack, she just left." "Oh, with who?" "His name is Jesse and I'm sorry but I'm not sure just when they'll be back. They haven't seen each other in a long time. They have quite a bit of uh, catching up to do. I'll be sure to tell her you called Jack." "Uh, No! That's okay. I don't want her to think I'm checking up on her or anything. I'll see her tomorrow at rehearsal. Goodnight." "Alright, goodnight Jack."

Jack tried to go to sleep but every time he closed his eyes he saw the two of them in that embrace and that *kiss*. "Yeah, I'll bet they have a lot of catching up to do. But why does it have to be with MY girlfriend?" He finally had to get out, so he decided to go for a long walk to clear his head. He got dressed and left his apartment.

A few minutes after he left, the phone rang. Lynetta was trying to reach him. When Jack didn't answer his home phone she called his cell phone but Jack had been so upset he didn't bother to take it with him. When he didn't answer either phone Lynetta began to worry. She waited a bit and called again...nothing. Jack wandered and wandered until he found himself at a small lake front. So he sat down and stared at the water. Lately the nights had been getting colder and Jack had left home without a jacket. There was quite a chilly wind coming off of that water. Lynetta decided he was sleeping heavily and couldn't hear either phone so she went on to bed. "I'll try again in the morning",she thought.

As the sun began to rise Jack realized he'd been out there staring at the water all night and had gotten <u>no</u> sleep at all. How could he go to rehearsal with no sleep? For that matter how could he go to rehearsal and see Lynetta without being reminded of what he saw at the Mall. "Am I losing her to someone else? What could I have done to push her away and into someone else's...arms?"(He thought). He decided to go home and shower and go to rehearsal anyway. But after he showered and dressed he didn't feel well. He felt like the room was spinning. Suddenly everything went black.

At rehearsal everyone was there but Jack. Danny asked, "Where is Jack?" But nobody knew. Now Lynetta was really worried. She thought, "There was no answer when I called last night, no answer when I called this morning. Where is Jack? Has something happened to him?"

She went over to Leon, "Did you see Jack after you played hoops yesterday?" "No!" "Did you talk to him?" "No!" Then Leon asked sarcastically, "Did you *enjoy yourself* at the Mall yesterday?" She looked at him oddly and replied, "Sure, I love to shop for new clothes. Wait a minute, how did you know I was at the Mall yesterday? I never said *where* we were going shopping." Leon said *hesitantly*, "We saw you there."

Lynetta said, "You did? I didn't see you." "How could you? You were kind of...*busy* at the time." "What do you mean I was *busy* at the time?" "After playing hoops we went to the Mall for some cold drinks and..." Lynetta interrupted, "What?" "We saw you...with your arms around some guy and you were...kissing." "And Jack saw it too?" "Uh... yeah, he did. Then he got upset and took off."

"Oh NO? He didn't. Leon, it's all a misunderstanding. It's not what you think! It's not what it looked like. It was just my friend Jesse. He's always teasing me that way. It was a joke. Does Jack think I was cheating on him?"

"I think so! It looked pretty real to him. I told Jack he should talk to you about it. But he couldn't deal with it so he just left. I didn't see him or talk to him after that."

"Leon, I called last night, twice and again this morning, there was no answer at either number. I'm worried will you call, PLEASE?" "Okay." Leon called Jack but no answer. Lynetta said in a worried voice, "Leon, I have to know! I'm going to his place." He could tell just how worried she was by the sound of her voice and by how hard she was shaking so he said, "You'd better come with me, you're in <u>no</u> condition to drive! I'm a little worried myself. Let's go!"

Before they left they went to Danny to let him know what was going on, "Danny, Jack hasn't answered either phone since last night and it's not like him to not answer his cell phone it's a private number, so Lynetta and I are going to his place to find out why." Danny said, "Good idea. Call me when you find him. He's a good kid, I hope nothing bad has happened!"

Leon took a firm hold of Lynetta's arm and they left quickly. A few minutes later they had arrived at Jack's apartment. His car was there but he didn't answer the bell. They'd been trying all the way over on the cell but there was still no answer.

Lynetta said, "Leon I just know...something bad..." Her voice trailed off. They went to the apartment manager and begged him to let them in to see if he was okay. But by now Lynetta was *certain* something was very wrong. The manager opened the door and they rushed in to find Jack lying on the floor, out cold and burning up with fever.

The Manager said, "I'll call 911, someone should get a blanket..." but Lynetta was already covering him up, (something she learned in her First Aid Training). In a rather worried voice, Lynetta said, "Jack, don't do this. Wake up, please!"

In minutes the ambulance arrived to take Jack to the hospital. Lynetta said, "I have to go with him Leon. I feel that this is all my fault." Leon said, "Go! I'll call Danny and fill him in then I'll meet you at the hospital. Hang in there and be strong...for Jack's sake. See you soon!" The ambulance took Jack and Lynetta to the hospital.

Hospital E.R. Nurse, "He has a raging fever with a temp of 104 degrees. How long has he had this high a fever?" Lynetta said, "I don't know. Maybe since late last night?" "I won't lie to you. If his temperature continues to climb and we don't get it down soon, he could be in real trouble. Now if you'll excuse me I'll see about tending to...(she looked at the paper on the clipboard she held) Jack."

Lynetta began to cry. Just then Leon walked in. He saw Lynetta in tears and went over to console her. Lynetta said, "This is all my fault. If he dies..." Leon said to Lynetta, "He's not going to die. He's very ill but he's NOT going to die! Stop thinking that. Come here." Leon wrapped his arms around Lynetta and she cried on his shoulder. "That's it. You just let it all out. I'm here for you Lynetta." He gently rocked her back and forth while lightly stroking her hair.

Just then Alyssa and Adrianne entered the E.R. They were surprised to see Leon's arms wrapped around Lynetta with her face now buried in his chest. Adrianne's mouth dropped open in shock. Leon looked over and saw Dre, then he looked at Lynetta and suddenly said, "This is NOT what it looks like." Adrianne quickly said, "What, a friend consoling a friend?" "Well, yeah if *that's* what it looks like."

Lynetta looked up and they saw she'd been crying. The girls took Lynetta over to a chair so she could sit for awhile. Adrianne said, "Thanks Leon for being here for her and taking such good care of her. How is Jack doing?"

"The nurse said he's <u>very</u> sick. But, he <u>has</u> to be alright...for her sake, (he nodded in Lynetta's direction). But Lynetta won't leave Jack's side for a second. I'm worried about her Dre!" Adrianne asked, "Leon, what happened to Jack? How did he get like this?"

Leon said to her, "All I can say right now is something Jack saw yesterday upset him a lot and he just took off. The next thing I know Lynetta and I found him on his apartment floor, out cold and burning up and now here we are at the hospital." "Yesterday you guys went to play hoops, right? What could he have seen that would have upset him so much?"

"After playing hoops we were thirsty, so we decided to go get some cold drinks. We went to the Food Court at the Mall. We came around the corner and..." "And what?" "Jack saw Lynetta kissing and hugging another guy."

"Wait, you guys saw that?" "Yeah, we did." "Leon why didn't you guys say anything before now? What you saw was all an act between two friends that have known each other...for a very long time."

Leon said, "Wait, we only saw Lynetta with this guy, were you and Lyssa there too?" "Yes Leon! We were in the Food Court talking to Blaine while Jesse was playing his little joke on Lynetta. She was completely taken by surprise." Leon said, "Obviously she wasn't the only one."

Adrianne said to Alyssa, "We have to get Lynetta out of here." "That isn't going to be so easy." Dre said, "I know but we have to try." The girls went over to Lynetta and tried to convince her to go get some rest but she couldn't or wouldn't. All she would say was, "This is all my fault, all my fault, my fault..."

Just then, their director, friend and mentor- Danny walked in... "Hey kids, how is Jack?" Leon filled him in, "He's not so good Danny and what's worse is we can't get Lynetta to leave his side for even a minute, and she's exhausted. I don't want to see her collapse but I don't know how much more she can take. And she keeps blaming herself."

Danny said, "Let me see what I can do. Sometimes age has its advantages." (He walked over to Lynetta and put his arm around her,)

"Hey kiddo, how are you?" Lynetta looked up at Danny and said, "Oh Danny this is ALL my fault!" (she sobbed) Danny said, "Hey now, it's going to be alright, you'll see. He's getting the <u>best</u> of care right now. BUT, if you don't get some rest you won't be any good to Jack and we'll be visiting <u>you</u> in the hospital instead of him. So, I want you to go with Adrianne and Alyssa, find a quiet place to sit or lie down and just rest." Lynetta said, "I can't. I have to be here if he wakes up. I have to explain to him what he really saw."

"Jack isn't going anywhere anytime soon and someone will come and get you when he's better or at least awake. Okay?" "Okay, Danny if you say so. I trust..." with that Lynetta collapsed from pure exhaustion, physical and emotional. Danny caught her... "NURSE!" They put her on a stretcher and Danny told them she was just exhausted and had only fainted." Danny said, "I need to call Jack's and Lynetta's parents. They should be here at a time like this."

The parents were called. Lynetta's mom arrived first just as Lynetta was coming to, "Hi honey. I'm here." Lynetta cried, "Oh mom...(she began) It's all my fault..." Mrs. H. calmly said, "There, there. I'm sure it's not as black as it seems. Jack is a strong and healthy young man. He'll get through this, you'll see. And you'll be there to help him I'm sure. But you can't let yourself get run down. When he's better you two will sit down and talk things out and be closer than ever. Now let's go get you something to eat so Jack can get his rest." Lynetta knew her mom was right, so she let them take her down for a bite to eat. "Thanks mom." She just smiled and gave Lynetta a hug.

Everyone took turns being with Jack so he would never be without at least one of his closest friends nearby, for Lynetta's sake. It was nearly midnight when Jack's fever finally broke. His temp was now down to under 100 degrees. Lynetta was so exhausted that she had slept for several hours. Alyssa said softly, "Lynetta, I think Jack's coming to. His fever finally broke." Lynetta woke up and went over to him. She took his hand in hers and with her other hand began to caress his face. As he slowly came to he couldn't believe his eyes. He looked up and there was Lynetta looking down at him with tears in her eyes.

"I'm so sorry I hurt you Jack. Can you ever forgive me?" He reached up to wipe her tears away. With a raspy voice he said, "It's you? I can't believe it, you're really here?(he cupped her face with his hand) I thought I had lost you! When I saw you with that other guy...?" "There is no <u>other</u> guy. I love YOU and <u>only</u> you. You have to believe that."

"Oh come here baby, I'm sorry I put you through all that. It's hard to believe I could be so jealous. I'm just so glad you're still my girl." Lynetta said, "I'm glad you still want me to be your girl."

Everyone was so relieved when Jack was released to go home. His parents wanted him to come home with them but he assured them he was fine and was going back to his place. "I know someone who will take very good care of me!" And he winked at Lynetta as she smiled back at him. When he was well again, Jack and Lynetta had a long talk, (as her mom suggested), and straightened everything out. After that their relationship was truly stronger and better than ever.

# _Three_

# _(Part 1)_
# _A Special Girl Named Ally_

It was Friday afternoon about 3:45 p m and everyone had been working hard at rehearsal. Danny addressed the cast, "Alright people, great job. Now, let me see one final run through of this number and we can all go home. It's Friday so lets get it done and get out of here. Ready and 5,6,7,8..."

The cast finished the number and Danny was very pleased. Everyone gave a loud cheer and Danny dismissed everyone for the weekend. "Great job everyone. I'm very impressed. Now, get out of here and have a terrific weekend. I'll see you all bright and early Monday morning, 6 a. m."

Leon, Jack and Brian headed out of the studio. Not far behind were Adrianne, Alyssa and Lynetta. The guys were talking about going out to a movie or staying in with a movie. Brian got an idea. "Hey, I know! It's Friday and *most* people wanna go out Friday night, but honestly, I just don't want to deal with all the crowds of people. If you guys want to go out I'll go along. I just thought it would be nice to have a quiet, enjoyable night in."

Leon said, "But what about the *girls* Brian?" "Oh, I wouldn't mind having the girls around, (Brian smiled)". Jack said, "You know I agree with Brian. A quiet night in, away from all the crowds does sound really nice and relaxing. Sitting with your arm around your favorite girl."

Leon said, "Okay, so who's going to ask the girls?" (Jack and Brian looked at each other and they both pointed to Leon.) Leon looked at them and said, "Wait a minute that's not fair." Jack said, "Why not? You just asked who was going to ask the girls?" So, Leon gave in, "Okay, you win. So who's place are we going to?"

Jack said, "You can all come over to my place, I have plenty of room *and* I just got a brand new, big screen T.V. with surround sound. It would be perfect. Now what do you guys want to do about dinner? Should we invite the girls for dinner and movies or invite them for just movies after dinner?"

Brian said, "Let's order Chinese takeout and have the girls over for dinner and a movie." Jack and Leon agreed, "That's a *great* idea!" The girls were standing by their cars talking when Leon walked up to them, "Hi, girls." "Hi, Leon." "Hey, I was talking with the guys about what we were going to do tonight. How would you girls like to join us at Jack's place for some Chinese takeout and a movie? Jack said he just got a brand new big screen T.V. with surround sound. So, how about coming over tonight?" The girls all looked at each other and they all agreed. Adrianne said, "Thank you Leon, we'd love to. What time?" He said, "How about 6:00?" She said, "Okay, see you at six." Leon said, "Alright!"

Then he went back over to the guys...! "Okay, it's all set. They're coming over at 6:00. Let's go." The guys and girls each went home to shower and get ready for their fun night together.

It was almost six when Leon arrived with the food. "Hey Jack where's Brian?" "He's not here yet. You're the first one." Just then someone honked. Leon yelled out, "It's the girls." Leon went out to meet them. "Hi Adrianne." "Hi Leon." Alyssa and Lynetta said, "Hey are we invisible or what?" "Oh, sorry. Hi Lyssa, Hi Lyn, has anyone seen Brian?" "Why? He's not here yet?" "No." Adrianne said, "I'm sure he'll be here soon. You know how much he loves Chinese takeout! Besides Leon, you said, Chinese takeout was his idea." "Well, let's go on in."

Meanwhile at Brian's apartment...Just as Brian was coming home from rehearsal and was getting out of his car he saw something across the parking lot. As he walked to his apartment he noticed a girl on the sidewalk who had apparently fallen, so he went over to her. He said to her, "Here let me help you." She said, "Thanks."

He helped her to her feet, but she couldn't stand very well. Suddenly she said, "Here boy." Just then a golden retriever peeked around Brian with something white in his mouth. He gently nudged Brian as if to say, "Here take this." (It was her cane.) He seemed to know Brian was there to help. Brian said to the dog, "Hey boy is she your master? She'll be okay." He took the cane and looped it over his wrist. Then he said to the dog, "Good boy!"

Brian looked around and saw a bench. Then he said to her, "I'm going to put you on this bench over here." So Brian picked her up and carried her over to the bench and tended to her ankle. "Oh no, your ankle is bleeding. I have a First Aid kit in my car. I'll be right back." Brian went for the First Aid kit and came back.

"Now let's see that ankle," he said. Brian cleaned and bandaged her ankle and then she tried again to stand up. But, when she started to put weight on that ankle it buckled and Brian caught her.

He told her, "I'm not sure, but, I think you sprained it. You should soak it and then wrap it when you get home." She said, "Great! Just what I need." Brian said, "Is there someone I can call for you? By the way, I don't even know your name. I'm Brian." "I'm Allyson, but you can call me Ally. And this is Sammy, my faithful companion." "Well nice to meet you both. Now, who can I call for you?" "Oh I have my cell phone...somewhere." "Uh, I'm afraid it broke when you fell."

"Oh no, I really should call my mom." Brian got out his cell phone. "What's the number?" "Oh, that's okay. I'll call later." Sounding a tad upset Brian said, "Now wait a minute, I just bandaged your ankle and carried you all the way over to this bench, now the least you could do is to let me call your mom so she doesn't worry. You can use my phone."

"Well since you put it that way and you have been very nice..." "And if that's not enough, Sammy here trusts me." "Okay." Ally gave Brian the phone number and he called her mom.

The phone was ringing, just then Ally's mom answered, "Hello?" "Hi. My name is Brian and I have someone here who would like to speak to you." "Who?" Brian put the phone in Ally's hand.

"Hi mom." "Ally? What's wrong?" "Oh I just tripped over my own feet, again." "Are you okay?" "Yes. But, Brian and I think I sprained my ankle." "Who is Brian? Is he a,a..." "Mom it's okay, he's just a nice guy who happened to come along after I fell and helped me up off the ground. Not to mention he cleaned and bandaged my ankle."

"Should I call the police?" "No mom. If I was in any danger Sammy would let me know. Besides, Brian has been a total gentleman. (in a whisper- I'll tell you all about it at home.) Now will you please come get us?" "Okay, I'll be right there. Wait, *where are* you?"

"Ally told her mom how to get there and hung up the phone. In a few minutes her mom was there. Brian began to introduce himself, "Hi, Mrs..., I'm sorry, I just realized, I don't know your last name." She held out her hand and said, "I'm Mrs. Grayson." "I'm Brian, it's so nice to meet you. I've really enjoyed talking with Ally." "Well, it certainly is nice to meet such a gentleman. Well Ally, we'd better be going home. It's getting rather late."

"Brian said, "Here let me..." Brian picked up Ally and carried her to the van and carefully put her inside. Then he asked, "Ally, may I call you later?" "Sure, I'd like that (she gave him her number) and thanks for everything Brian." and she smiled at him.

Mrs. Grayson put Sammy in the van and turned to thank Brian. He replied, "Oh, you're welcome. I just happened along at the right time I guess." "Well thanks again! Goodbye." "Bye."

Brian waited until the van was out of sight to leave. Just then his cell phone rang, "Hello?" "Hey Brian where are you?" "Oh Jack, hey man I'm sorry, I'll be there as soon as I can and I'll explain everything." "What? What happened? Are you alright?" "Yeah, I'm fine! I'll tell you later. Bye." Brian hung up and went in to shower and change.

Then he jumped into his car and went to Jack's place. All Brian could think about was Ally. Soon he was pulling up to Jack's place. He got to the door, knocked and went in. "I'm sorry I'm so late. Something came up but here I am." Brian grabbed some food and a cola. He sat down by Adrianne and even though the conversation was lively Brian was deep in thought about Ally and lost in his own little world.

The guys tried to talk to him, "Okay Brian? Brian?" Then all 5 at once shouted, "**BRIAN!**" Brian shook his head and snapped out of his trance, "What?" Jack said, "Hey man, where did you just go?" Brian said, "Nowhere."Leon said, "So are we ready to start the movie?" Jack said, "I am. Let's do it." Jack put the movie in and they all sat down to watch it.

Soon after the movie began Brian drifted off again into "Ally-land". He just couldn't get her off of his mind. He let his thoughts drift back to when he arrived home and he looked over and saw someone on the ground. He was in a little bit of a hurry and was just going to go inside to shower and change but something made him walk over to check it out.

When he got over to her, he took one look at her and that was all it took. She was beautiful! She had long, chestnut brown hair that went all the way to her waist. Then she turned her face to look up at him with the most gorgeous, sparkling, emerald green eyes he had ever seen. Then when she smiled at him, it made his heart pound so hard he was sure she could hear it...!

Suddenly he noticed someone was shaking him. It was Leon. "Okay dude, spill it. What's with you tonight? You haven't been here, with us all night? And who is Ally?" Everyone was looking at him, so Brian decided to tell all of them, about Ally. "I met Ally today on my way home..."

After he finished Jack said, "So, when do we get to meet this girl that has you so mesmerized?"

Brian said, "Now wait a minute. I only met her today. It's not like we're dating or anything. She's just a girl, a girl I was able to help."

Leon said, " But dude, she must be something special, you haven't been able to get her off your mind all night. So why don't you ask her out?" Jack said, "Hey Brian, I think you should go for it. Even if she said no, at least you tried. But what if she said yes? You'll never know unless you ask her."

Brian said, "Well I did say I'd call her later, because I wanted to find out how her ankle was." Jack asked, "Does she know you were going to call about her ankle or just that you were going to call her? Brian just call her and talk to her. Believe me you'll be glad you did. Hey, it's only 8:00 go call her now!" Brian said, "Okay, okay." So Brian called Ally, "Hello?" "Hi, Mrs Grayson? This is Brian, we met this afternoon." "Oh yes, Hello Brian. How are you?" "Fine thank you. How is Ally this evening?" "Oh she's fine. Would you like to talk to her?" "Yes I would, thank you." "Just a minute, (off in the distance; Ally telephone)."

Ally picked up the phone, "Hello?" "Hi Ally, it's Brian, How are you? And how's your ankle?" "Oh Hi, I'm fine. My ankle's a bit sore but the doctor said it isn't broken just a sprain, like you said. How' d you know it was a sprain?" "Well from time to time a dance... a ball player can get a slight sprain if he lands wrong." "Oh, you're a ball player. What kind of ball do you play?" "Basketball. Well I'd better let you get your rest so your ankle can heal. You know I really did like the short time we spent together today, only..." "Only what?" "It was too short. I would like to see you again." "I'd like that. How about tomorrow?" "That would be great! I can come over after lunch. How does 1:00 sound?" "Terrific, my mom can tell you how to get here. See you tomorrow." "Okay, until tomorrow then."

Ally's mom gave Brian directions to their house and hung up. Brian was on "cloud 9"! Leon punched Jack lightly in the shoulder and the two smiled and nodded at each other. Jack said, "I can't wait to meet this girl. She's sent Brian into orbit! Leon said, " No kidding she must be something else!" Brian said, "Oh she IS!  She definitely  IS!!" The girls said, "Go Brian!" and smiled.

Adrianne said, " Well it's about time you had a special lady in your life. You're a cool guy Brian, you deserve it." Brian said, "Well, I think I'll call it a night. See you guys tomorrow morning. We are still going to shoot hoops in the morning, right?" "Sure if you want to." "See you on the court." Brian went home and soon after, everyone else did the same.

In the morning the guys met at the B-ball court to shoot some hoops.  Jack said, "So, Brian are you going to see Ally today?" Brian said, "Yep, 1:00, right after lunch." Leon said, "Let us know when we get to meet the little lady." Jack said, "Yeah dude, I can't wait. I told you that last night."

It was 12:00 noon when the guys broke for lunch. Brian said, "Thanks guys, that was fun! Gotta go now. I'll catch ya later." Leon and Jack both said, "Okay, later dude."

Brian went home, had lunch, showered and changed. Then he headed for Ally's house, But first, the flower shop. Brian picked out a small bouquet of brightly colored assorted flowers and a get well card. He went on over to Ally's house and knocked on the door, (knock knock). Mrs. Grayson answered, "Oh, Hi Brian, it's nice to see you again. Come on in, Ally's in the family room." She took him back to see Ally.

"Hi Brian, thanks for coming over." "Hi, how are you?" "Fine. I'm just so bored I can't stand it. I've listened to my    I-POD about 1,000 times. I wish I could take Sammy for a walk." Brian said, "Why don't we? Oh, by the way, these are for you." (he pulled the flowers from behind his back.) "Oh Brian they're beautiful. She called to her mom, "Mom", (her mom came in to see what she wanted.) "What is it Ally?" "Look what Brian brought for me." "How lovely, here, let me put those in some water."

Brian said, "I know you probably can't see it much less read it but I got you a card and I thought you could at least see the colors and I can read it to you, it says, Dear Ally, Please get well soon so I can take you out on a proper date, if you'll let me. Brian. Here, hold out your hand." Brian put the card in her hand so she could see the bright colors.

"Oh Brian, It's almost as pretty as the flowers themselves. Thank you so much. You're so thoughtful." "Now how about that walk with Sammy?" "But I can't walk." "No, but I know you have a wheelchair and all *you* have do is hold Sammy's leash and I can push you. You could use some fresh air. You're too pretty to look as pale as you do. Let's get you some sunshine." "Okay. You're the boss."

Ally's mom was a little worried but she hadn't seen her daughter this happy in quite a long time and for some reason she trusted Brian. It was a warm afternoon but mom insisted Ally take her sweater along just in case it turned cold. Brian assured her Ally was in good hands and he said she could call them on his cell phone if she got too worried. With that said, out the door the three of them went.

They were gone for nearly and hour and her mom had resisted calling. Just as she was about to call Brian's cell, she heard voices at the front door. She looked out to see the two of them playing ball with Sammy. Feeling quite relieved, Mrs Grayson smiled and went to the kitchen to make some lemonade. She took it out to Ally and Brian. "Would you two like some lemonade?" Ally and Brian said, "Sure." Ally said, "Thanks Mom."

Mrs Grayson couldn't believe the difference in how Ally looked. Could Brian be the difference? Ally had such a glow about her and she looked so happy. Just then Ally began to yawn. Brian said, "I think I'd better get you inside. You've had quite a busy day and I don't want to make you over tired."

So Brian took her inside. He picked her up from her chair and put her on the couch so carefully. Ally said, " Don't go Brian." He said, "Are you sure? You look so tired." Ally replied, "But it's a good kind of tired."

Her mom said, "Ally could I see Brian for a minute?" "Okay, Mom." Brian said, "I'll be right back." Then he squeezed her hand just before he went in to see what her mom wanted. "What is it Mrs. G?"

"Brian, I'm grateful for all the care you've given Ally but I'm concerned about her emotional well being. To put it simply, I don't want to see her get hurt. You took care of her when she got hurt and then did a wonderful follow up to... check on how well she was doing, but now I think it's time for you to move on. I think Ally needs to get back to her reality."

Brian said, "What do you mean '*her reality*'? Does that mean I can't see her any more? Mrs Grayson, I like Ally. I think she likes me. We enjoy spending time together. What's wrong with that?" Mrs. Grayson said, "I just don't want her to become too emotionally attached to someone who...may not be around very long."

Brian said, "I think Ally is mature enough to decide who she wants to spend her time with and how much time. It's not like we're talking marriage. We're *just* friends." Mrs. Grayson said, " Okay Brian, as long as that's all it is?"

Brian said, "It is...for now. We'll see what the future holds when the time comes. As for Ally, I wouldn't hurt her for anything." Mrs Grayson gently said, "Well since you put it that way, I'm glad you're here for my daughter. I'm sorry if I sounded, well, harsh. It's just when it comes to Ally..." "It's okay. I understand. She's your daughter and you have to protect her." "I'm glad you understand. Would you like to stay for dinner?" Brian said, "I don't want to intrude." Mrs. Grayson said, "Oh you won't be and besides I know Ally would love to have you stay." Brian said, "In that case I'd love to. But maybe we should check with the *boss*?" (he glanced in Ally's direction.)

Mrs. Grayson said, "Oh Ally, should we have Brian stay for dinner?" "Oh could we? Please?" Mrs. Grayson said, "Well, there you are. Will you stay?" "Okay, you have a dinner guest. Thank you."

As soon as it was ready they all sat down to dinner and talked and laughed till way into the night. Then the conversation began to die down. Ally was getting sleepy. She was starting to nod off.

Mrs. Grayson said, "I'd better get Ally to bed." Brian said "Here, let me!" Brian picked Ally up and followed her mom to Ally's room and he put her to bed. He covered her up and kissed her forehead then he whispered, "Goodnight Ally."

He then said to her mom, "Thank you Mrs. Grayson for such a wonderful day. I don't remember when I've had such a great time." Mrs. Grayson said, "I'm glad you came over. It was a joy having you. Please come back again, anytime." Brian said, "Thanks, I'd like that! Goodnight!" Mrs. Grayson said, "Goodnight Brian!"

Brian went home feeling so happy. He couldn't remember the last time he felt this happy. He knew it was all because of Allyson and thought about her all the way home. When he got home he went straight to bed, closed his eyes and whispered, "Goodnight Ally", then he fell asleep.

# Three

## (Part 2)
## Adrianne Steps in to Help

It was Sunday morning 6 a. m. and Brian was wide awake! He thought, "I probably shouldn't call the guys, it's too early. Think I'll take a walk." He got dressed and went out for awhile. When he got home there was a message waiting for him, "Hi Brian, it's Ally. When you hear this call me back. I'll be waiting to hear from you." That's what he wanted to hear. So he called her back.

"Hello, Grayson residence." Brian in a concerned voice, "Ally? What's wrong?" She replied, "Nothing really, I just wanted to hear your voice. I didn't mean to worry you, sorry." "Oh that's okay. I don't know if I was actually worried or just excited to hear that you wanted me to call you back. But I _am_ glad that you're alright."

Ally asked, "What are you doing this morning? And have you had breakfast yet?" "I just went for a walk and no, no breakfast yet, why?" "Well, they're having breakfast at my church this morning around 8:00 and I thought you might like to go with us, so I called to invite you. Would you like to go?" Brian was rather hesitant about answering,

"Oh, *Church*. I guess we never did discuss religion or *anything* too deeply, did we?" "No we haven't. You don't *have* to go if you don't want to, it's your choice. I just thought it would be fun to go together." (she tried to keep the disappointment out of her voice).

Brian replied, "Well, I'd really rather not. I'm sorry. I'm just not very big on going to church. But, can I see you later?"

"I don't know. Well I have to go now. We'll talk later." "I'd like that. Ally? Are you alright? You sound... I don't know, *different*." "Different, how?" (I hope he'll change his mind.)

"I don't know exactly. A little down, maybe?" Ally replied quickly, "Oh, I'm probably just a little tired still from yesterday. It was longer than I realized until I went to bed. But, I'll be okay" "Okay, if you're sure, we'll talk later." "I'm sure! Bye now." "Bye Ally."

After Brian hung up the phone he thought, "Something just doesn't feel right. There was an odd sound in Ally's voice after I refused her invitation to...wait a minute, was it her invitation to breakfast or the "*church*" thing?" He decided to just dismiss it. He'd talk to her later and straighten it out.

Brian decided since he'd gotten up early, that he'd go back to bed and get some more sleep. So he went to lie down but the sound of Ally's voice kept him tossing and turning. He finally got up about noon and thought he should have some lunch. But he wasn't hungry.

Brian thought, "I wonder if she's back from church yet? Maybe she'll call." He waited and waited. "It's 2 p. m. She hasn't called yet. Well, I'm the *guy*, maybe she's a little "old fashioned" and is waiting for me to call her. Okay, I can do that.

He called, "Hello? Grayson residence." "Hi. Mrs. Grayson, it's Brian, may I speak to Ally please?" "Oh, I'm sorry Brian she's busy and can't talk just now. Maybe later?" Brian said, "Okay, will you tell her I called?" "Sure, bye now." "Bye Mrs. Grayson"

Adrianne called up Brian in a bubbling voice, "Hey Brian, how are you?" "Oh, I'm okay, how are you?" "Hey, what's wrong Brian? And don't say nothing, I can hear it in your voice. Talk to me."

He didn't answer. "Would you like me to come over so we can talk?" "I don't know I'm not very good company right now. Maybe you'd better not." "Let me be the judge of that. It sounds like you could use a friend right now. I'll come over and we'll see how it goes. Then if you want me to leave I will." Brian said in a depressing tone, "Whatever you want to do..." "Okay Brian! That's IT. I'll be right over."

A few minutes later Adrianne arrived at Brian's. "Hi Brian." "Hi Adrianne." "Is this the same Brian who just last Friday night was way out in orbit on CLOUD 9? What happened between then and today to make you this down? Come on Brian, talk to me. I'm here to help if you'll let me." "Okay. Here it is..." Brian told Adrianne everything that happened right up until she called. "Brian, how much do you know about Ally's religious background?" "Not much. I guess you could say not anything really." "Then it sounds like you need to get to know her better and a lot more about her." "But I can't if she won't talk to me." "Do you want *me* to talk to her for you, at least to get the two of you talking?" "Would you?" "Sure, just give me her phone number." "Thank you Dre."

Adrianne called Ally for Brian, "Hello?" "Hi could I talk to Ally please?" "Who's calling?" "Adrianne." "Just a minute...Ally- telephone." Ally answered, "Hello?" "Hi Ally. You don't know me, I'm Adrianne a friend of Brian's." "Oh, Hi Adrianne, Brian has told me so much about you and his other friends, Jack and Lynetta and Leon..., any way, what can I do for you?"

"Tell me why you won't talk to Brian. He doesn't understand and frankly, neither do I. You know, he really likes you. If there is a problem Ally, the only way you and Brian can fix it is to talk about it. Sweeping it under the rug or ignoring it doesn't make it go away. Right now my friend Brian is very depressed and if *he* is I'm sure *you* are too. Please say you'll talk to him?" Ally said, "Alright, Brian may come over for a short visit." "Thank you Ally. Goodbye."

Adrianne turned towards Brian and said, "Okay Brian, tonight you are going over to Ally's and talk things out!" "Thanks Adrianne you're a great friend. I owe you a big one!" "Hey, friends help each other, right?" "Right. Well I guess I'd better go over now before I lose my nerve." "Good Luck! Let me know how it went?" "I will. Thanks Dre!" and she went home.

Brian went to see Ally. When he got there he started to doubt himself. He called Adrianne on his cell- "Adrianne what am I doing here? What should I say?" "Brian what did you talk about when you met? Go back to that. Keep it simple. You can do this. Now go on and just do it!" "Thank you Adrianne."

Brian took a deep breath and rang the bell. Mrs. Grayson opened the door. "Hello Brian. Ally's in the family room. You can go on back."

He reached the family room and Ally's back was to him. "Ally? Hi. Can we talk? Please?" He tried to say it as gently as he could. He could tell she'd been crying. Ally nodded her head. He asked, "May I sit beside you?" Again she nodded.

Brian said, "You know this is going to be a strange conversation if I'm doing *all* the talking." Just then Ally let out a small chuckle. She turned her head slightly and he saw her face. "Did I cause those tears in those beautiful eyes? If I did, I'm so sorry! Talk to me Ally. Tell me, what's wrong?"

She hesitated a bit then she softly said, "I'm scared. I don't know where to begin." "Well, do you like me, as a friend?"

"Yes, at least I did, but now I don't know. I don't know what to think, or feel, or anything. I'm so confused." "It's the "church" thing, isn't it?" Ally nodded. "We were fine until that came up and I said no. Am I right?" She nodded again and Brian saw a tear fall and roll down her cheek. Just then she looked away.

"Now wait a minute. This isn't the end of the world. I just never gave church much thought. It always *seemed* to be something for old people, fanatics and people that don't seem to have a life." "You mean people like <u>me</u> because I'm partially blind, right?"

Brian knelt in front of Ally and took hold of both of her hands and said, "No, No, maybe I used to think of blind people that way but Ally you're <u>so</u> different! You're young, beautiful, alive and so full of energy that I almost have to remind myself that..."

"That I'm blind? Yes! I AM BLIND! But- maybe I'm not the *only* one here that is *blind*. I have a handicap and sometimes that makes people *blind* to who <u>I</u> really am- *inside*. But I'm not afraid to show who I am, unlike some others." She tried to pull away but Brian wouldn't let go.

"Maybe that's what I liked best about you when we met?" "What do you mean?" "You said it yourself. <u>You're</u> not afraid to show who you really are. I think that's terrific!"

"But Brian, the problem is, it's a turnoff, *especially to guys*." "What is?" "Guys don't usually want a girl with a mind of her own. One who knows what she wants AND who,,,believes in God, there I said it. Church has always been a big part of my life and more so since my sight has gotten worse. But it's hard enough to get guys to see beyond the cane and the chair but when you add the church thing, that's when they all run. Things will go fine, just like with you, right up until I suggest going to church. Why can't I find a guy with whom I can share my religion and my life, who won't run away from me?" Ally began to cry.

"Now hold up one minute Ally Grayson, (Brian sounded a bit angry). If you'll remember, you're the one who wouldn't talk to me this afternoon. I called but your mom said you were too busy so I hung up. But I thought you'd at least call me back when you were free, so we could talk."

"Wait, you called earlier, today?" "Yeah, around 2:00." "I didn't know you called. No one ever told me." (Just then her mom walked past the doorway.)

"MOM !", (she shouted). Mrs. Grayson said, "Yes Ally?" "Why didn't you tell me Brian had called me earlier?" "Ally, we'll talk about it later." "No mom! We'll talk about it NOW! (Ally was getting more angry,) You owe me the truth mom and you owe Brian an apology. Admit it mom. You don't want Brian and me together, do you? I just realized something. Every guy who's wanted to spend any time with me, alone, suddenly seemed to be uninterested. I always thought it was me. But It's been you all along mom, hasn't it? How many others called back that you sent away? She didn't answer. Well?"

"Okay. Yes! Yes I did, for your own good. They weren't the right kind for you honey." "Don't you mean they weren't the kind of guy you had all picked out for me? Mom I'm 18. I can pick the kind of guy I want to date. The kind of guy I want may not measure up to your standards but mom, (Ally's voice softened,) you raised me with good, strong moral values. Trust that! And trust me and my judgment, please? I love you mom but sooner or later you'll have to let me go."

"I'm sorry Ally, Brian. Can you both forgive a silly old lady?" As a tear escaped the corner of her eye and slid down her cheek she said, "I just wanted what I thought was best for my daughter. I guess I forgot she was growing up into such a strong and smart young woman."

Brian said, "Mrs. Grayson you're just a caring mom looking out for her daughter's well being. I can see that. You'll always love her in a way no one else ever will. But, there are others who can love her too, if you give them a chance. Right now I like Ally, a lot and we may never be more than just friends but what's wrong with that? Everyone needs a good friend to lean on. Don't you think so?"

She nodded and said, "Brian, I'd be proud to call you my daughter's friend. Please come back. We'll both be happy to have you."

Ally smiled and squeezed Brian's hand, then she whispered, "Thanks Brian and thank Adrianne for me." "I will. It's late now. You should get some sleep. I don't want <u>my</u> girl all tired out. I'll call you tomorrow. I promise." He kissed Ally's forehead and left. By the time she realized *what* he had said he was already gone. She said to herself, "*my girl.*"

# Four

# Jarrod Walks Out on Alyssa

It's another Friday afternoon and it's been a long, tough week of rehearsals. Learning new stuff. Trying to remember everything that's thrown at them and hoping they're doing it right. According to Danny, everyone has been truly amazing.

Danny again addressed the cast, "Okay everyone, you're looking good. It's all coming together. I know it's been a tough week but you all came through for me. I like what I'm seeing. Once again it's Friday. Have a great weekend! See you all on Monday morning. You're dismissed, now get out of here!" he said with a smile.

Everyone headed for the parking lot. The gang looked over at the door and Alyssa walked out with Jarrod's arm around her.

Leon said, "Hey, check out the lovebirds." Adrianne said, "Chill out Leon. We all know they've been dating for quite awhile now." Leon said, "I know. But they're so much fun to tease. Especially Alyssa. She blushes so easily."

Then Jack said, "Yeah, but dude, if you're not careful, she can get really mad, really fast, and you *don't* want that. Repercussions can be really B A D."

Leon said, "Na, I can handle it." Jack said, "Yeah, but can you handle Jarrod when he comes to her rescue? And you know he will." Leon said, "Oh, forget it. I was only kidding. (Jack smiled) Hey, feel like shooting some hoops tonight?" Jack said, "Maybe? I don't have any plans *yet*."

Leon said, "Cool, I'll call you later. Maybe Brian and Jarrod would like to mix it up. I'll call and ask them. Later dude." Jack said, "Later."

Leon called Brian, "Hey Brian, you wanna go shoot some hoops with me and Jack tonight? I also thought I'd call and ask Jarrod if he wants to come over and mix it up, if he's not busy tonight."

Brian said, "I'm not sure, I thought I'd call up Ally and see if she wanted to do something tonight. I haven't seen her since Sunday. I'll call you back and let you know either way. Thanks Leon."

Leon called Jarrod, "Hey Jarrod, it's Leon. The guys are getting together tonight to shoot some hoops are you game?"

"I don't know Leon. I was thinking about taking Alyssa out but she looked so tired I'm not sure if she wants to or not. Can I call you back and let you know?" "Sure. Later."

Brian ended up going over to Ally's. Jarrod took a rain check and went over to Alyssa's. Lynetta and Adrianne were spending the night together doing girl stuff. So, Jack and Leon spent a couple of hours playing one on one. Finally the two took a break from B-ball for a soda. All of a sudden, both said at once, "Let's go check out the girls!" They had a good laugh, then Jack said, "let's go to my place and you can use my shower." Then Leon said, "I can't wear this! I'll just meet you at Lynetta's." "That's cool, dude. See you soon."

Lynetta and Adrianne just finished watching a movie and decided to do their nails. Adrianne said, "Girl this is so much fun! We should do this more. And maybe Alyssa can come next time?" "Yeah, if she's not too busy with Jarrod."

"Yeah but, you have to admit they do look good together. Just like you and Jack!" Lynetta just smiled shyly and blushed. She was easily embarrassed when people spoke about Jack and her.

Suddenly there was a knock on the door. The girls looked at each other with a puzzled look and both went to the door. Lynetta looked out of the peep hole. She turned toward Adrianne and whispered,

"Guess who." Then she said out loud, "Who is it?"

A voice answered, "Pizza Delivery!" Lynetta whispered to Adrianne, "Let's have some fun." Adrianne nodded in agreement. Then Lynetta said, firmly, "I'm sorry, you must have the wrong address. We didn't order a pizza." "Well maybe someone ordered it for you. This is the address I have. Why don't you just take a look and see?" "I don't know, I shouldn't open my door to a perfect stranger." (She smiled trying to keep from laughing.)

"Well I don't need any money. It's paid for. Please just take a look?" "I don't know." (The girls were just dying to laugh out loud.) "Please?!" Finally she gave in. "Well, okay." She opened the door to see Jack and Leon standing there smiling really big.

Pizza delivery huh? So where's the pizza? (she smiled at both of them.) They all had a good laugh. Jack looked at Lynetta and said, "Did you miss me?" She smiled shyly and blushed a little. He said, "You know you look so cute when you do that." He was still smiling at her.

"So what are you girls up to?", Leon asked. Adrianne said, "Not much just a bunch of girl stuff. What about you guys, other than delivering invisible pizza?" Jack answered, "Oh you know, more hoops. The more you play the better you get." As the conversation continued the group moved over to the living room where they all sat and talked awhile.

A little while later Jack asked Lynetta, "Would you like something more to drink?" She said, "Yes." Jack went to the kitchen and moments later Lynetta followed him. Jack turned around and suddenly he was face to face with her. All he could do was stand there and look at her. Then she took his hand and put it around her waist. He slid his other arm around her and pulled her close to him. She laid her head on his chest and he softly kissed her hair. As they stood cuddled together he didn't want to let her go. But Leon came in, cleared his throat and said, "Dude, we should go. It's late." Jack looked over at Leon and said, "I know dude, give us a minute." A few minutes later the guys said goodnight to the girls and headed for home.

The next morning the girls got up and had breakfast. They had decided to go for a run so they got ready and went outside to finish stretching. Someone let out a whistle so they looked up and...yes, you guessed it- Jack and Leon.

Jack asked, "And where are you lovely ladies going on this beautiful morning?" Lynetta replied, "We're going for a run. Wanna join us?" Jack said, "Sounds good to me. Let's go Leon." Leon said, "Okay. Let's do it." About 20 minutes into their run they came to a park.

Lynetta said, "Anyone for a little playtime in the park?" Jack said, "Yeah, I am, let's go." Lynetta tagged Jack and said, "You're it!" and took off running. Jack chased her, she dodged around the slide, "Missed me." "I'll get you!" Jack said. He stopped and hid. Lynetta looked around, no Jack. He sneaked around her. She wondered where he went when all of a sudden, "GOTCH YA!" He grabbed her around her waist and they fell to the ground laughing.

As they lay there Jack propped himself up on one elbow and looked into her eyes. Then he leaned over and kissed her. She said, "You're so sneaky."

Leon was pushing Adrianne on the swings. Lynetta looked at Jack and said, "That looks like fun." So they went over and joined Leon and Adrianne. When they'd had enough of the swings they all ran over to the merry-go-round. The girls got on and the guys got it going and jumped on. Finally the merry-go-round came to a stop and they all went for a slow walk across the park. They all headed back to Lynetta's house. Lynetta asked, "Would you guys like to come in for a cold drink?"

Jack and Leon both said, "Sure, thanks!" They all went into the kitchen and got their drinks. Lynetta suggested they go out on the deck and they did. The guys each sat in a deck chair so the girls could have the lounge chairs. The guys sort of slouched down in the chairs so they could put their heads back and close their eyes.

Meanwhile, Lynetta got Adrianne's attention. As she stood behind Jack and pointed to his shoulders Adrianne nodded in agreement and got behind Leon. Suddenly the girls began massaging the guys shoulders.

Jack let out a pleasurable moan and said, "Oh h, I love this!" Leon said, "Oh yeah! This is the life," and gave a pleasurable moan of his own.

After a few minutes Jack took Lynetta by the hand and said, "Come here you." and he gently pulled her over onto his lap. She looked at him and said, "But I'm not done with your shoulders yet" "Yeah you are. I want you right here, right now." He gently pulled her chin toward him and kissed her softly.

Leon tried the same thing with Adrianne but she was feeling a bit more playful so she started a tickling match with him. They were laughing so hard the tears were rolling down her face and Leon's sides were hurting. So they just sat and relaxed for a while to catch their breath.

Suddenly the phone rang. Lynetta picked it up and someone was crying on the other end. "Alyssa, is that you?"   "Yes." "Honey, what's wrong?" "Jarrod and I just had a big fight and he just walked out and left. I don't know what to do? I'm sure it was just a misunderstanding, but he was so angry."   "Alyssa, I want you to come over here tonight." "Are you sure?" "Yes. You're going to spend the night with us girls! Do you feel okay to drive over or should I have Jack come and get you?" "Is Jack there with you now?" "Yes." "Oh never mind, I'll be okay. I'll call you tomorrow..." Alyssa let out a sob then quickly hung up and then Lynetta really began to worry about her.

From the look on Lynetta's face Jack knew something was bothering her. "What is it babe?" She said, "Jack, Alyssa is really upset. She just had a big fight with Jarrod and he left very angry. I told her to come over but when she heard you were  here she said,  "Never mind" and hung up. I'm worried. Would you go over there and convince her to come over and drive her over here, please?

Jack said, "Sure! Tell you what. I'll bring her here and then Leon and I will see if we can find Jarrod to hear his side of it and maybe get this thing resolved quickly. Will she need to bring anything?" "Yes, a change of clothes. I have everything else. Thank you Jack, I can always count on you. You're wonderful."

"You know I'll do anything for you baby. I'll be back as soon as I can with Alyssa." He kissed her and with that he took off for Alyssa's.

Leon had heard what Jack had said to Lynetta and he told her, "Jack and I will leave as soon as he gets here with Alyssa."

Adrianne said, "I'll stay if you think I can help or would you rather talk to her alone?" "Let's ask Alyssa when she gets here." "Good idea."

Just then Jack pulled up with Alyssa. She came in, her eyes all red from crying. Jack brought her bag in and set it on the floor. He turned toward Alyssa, took hold of her shoulders and told her, "Alyssa, whatever happened I'm sure you two can work it out and the two of you will be back together very soon. You need to believe that." "Thank you Jack. I hope so. I don't know what I'd do without him.''

Jack and Leon said their goodbyes and took off to look for Jarrod.

Adrianne said to Alyssa, "Do you want to talk to Lynetta alone? Cause I'll take off too, if you want." But Alyssa said, "Well I don't want you to have to leave because of me." "No, no, Alyssa. I'll give you two some time alone to talk and if you want to talk to me, just call me and I'll be right here, okay?"

"Thanks Adrianne for being so understanding. You and Lynetta are the best friends I could have."

Adrianne said, " Aw, what are friends for? I'll be at home if you need me." She gave Alyssa a big hug and left.

Jack said to Leon, "Hey man where do you think we should look for Jarrod?" Leon asked, "Where does he usually hang out?" "The Coffee Shoppe for one, The Pier or maybe The Bistro, if he's not just hangin' at his place. He should be at one of those places." "Okay dude, let's go."

They looked in a couple of places and found him drowning his sorrows in Espresso.

Jack said, "Hey Jarrod, What's up dude?" "Oh hi guys." "So, what's new with you?" "Alyssa and I just had a huge fight so I took off to clear my head."

Leon said, "Yeah, she looked pretty shaken up dude. That must have been some fight. What happened?" "I'm not really sure. We were doing just fine, then I said something and she just got all mad and then we were yelling at each other so I got up and left before I could say anything to make it worse."

Jack asked, "Do you remember what you said right before she got mad?" Jarrod said, " No. I keep going over the whole thing in my head and I don't get it."

Meanwhile, at Lynetta's, Alyssa was still very upset. Alyssa said, "I don't know what I said to make him so mad or what he said to make me so mad but we were yelling at each other just before he walked out. I don't even know if he still loves me or not?"

"Lyssa, do you still love Jarrod?" "Yes, of course I do. I want him back. I'll do anything." "Okay, here's our plan of action..."

Back with the guys, Jack asked Jarrod, "Do you still love Alyssa?" "Yes, of course I do." "When was the last time you told her that?" "I don't know, last week, maybe? She knows I love her."

Leon added, "Dude, we're talking about girls here. It doesn't matter whether they know it, they need to hear it and that means..."

Jack jumped in with, "You HAVE TO SAY IT ! And say it often. At least once a day or more. If you don't they think you don't care or worse, that you don't love them any more. They might even begin to think there's someone else? Is there someone...?" "Not for me. Alyssa's the only one I want. I just can't figure her out sometimes, you know?"

Leon said, "So don't try to. Just tell her what she wants and needs to hear. Believe us you'll see a difference. A BIG difference." Jack said, "Now, what is Alyssa's favorite kind of flower, Roses, Carnations, a variety? Get a small bunch and a small box of chocolates too, especially if you had a really big fight. Now, tonight you should take her to HER favorite restaurant and order her favorite menu item or let her pick it out. Remember when you first started dating Alyssa and go from there." "I remember I got..." Jarrod started remembering his first few dates with Alyssa.

Back with the girls, Lynetta called Adrianne, "Adrianne? It's Lynetta, come back to my place. I'll need your help. We are going to do a makeover on Alyssa." "Cool! I'll be right over!" Alyssa showered and began to get ready. Adrianne arrived, "Okay, I'm here!" Lynetta said, "Okay girls, let's go to Alyssa's and finish the job."

They got to Alyssa's and she put on the dress Jarrod loves to see her in, (the short simple black one with the ruffled skirt). Then the girls did her hair and makeup.

The girls stood back when everything was done, they looked at each other and back at Alyssa, in unison they said,"WOW!" Then Adrianne added, "Girl, you're gonna knock- him- out!"

Jack realized the girls didn't know their plans. He thought, "What if they take off with Alyssa somewhere? I'd better call Lynetta and see what's going on." Lynetta answered her cell, "Hello?" "Hi baby, it's Jack, How is Alyssa?" "Oh, hi Jack. She's much better, thanks. It was sweet of you to call and check on her. Any luck finding Jarrod?"

"Is she there with you now?" "Yes. Why Jack?" " I need you to take the phone somewhere so we can talk privately. Alyssa can't hear what you're saying, understand?" "Okay, just give me a second."

"Lyssa I'll be right back." Lyn returned to her phone call with Jack, "Okay go." "Leon and I went to find Jarrod after we left your place. We were both sure it was just a huge misunderstanding. We found him and talked him into making up with Alyssa. So I was thinking he should take her to her favorite restaurant and take it from there. (Lynetta chuckled) What's so funny?" "I was going to call Jarrod to suggest to him that he should do just that."

"Now I know why I love you so much baby. You're terrific! Okay, so you're at your house right?" "Uh, no, actually it's a good thing you called. We're at Alyssa's." "Alyssa's?" "Yeah, we did a make over so we decided to do it here with her stuff. Oh Jack, you should see her. She looks like..., she looks great!"

"Okay, then, I'll send Jarrod to Alyssa's. See you soon." "Thanks baby." Pretty soon Jarrod pulled up. He rang the bell and Lynetta answered, "Hi Jarrod, wow, don't you look nice." "Thanks. Is Alyssa here?" "Sure. Come on in. I'll be right back." Lyn went into the other room and called, "Alyssa? Someone's here to see you."

Alyssa walked into the room and Jarrod's mouth dropped open. "WOW! You... you look stunning. You, you take my breath away. Oh baby I'm so sorry about this afternoon. It was all my fault. Here, these are for you but they look pale compared to you."

"Oh Jarrod, they're beautiful, Thank you. I'm sorry too. It was a simple misunderstanding and we both blew it way out of proportion. Can you forgive me? I love you so much."

"I love you too and I'm going to tell you that as often as I can so you'll always know how much I love my Alyssa. Can I take you to dinner?" "Yes, I'd like that." "You're so beautiful. Here, I want you to take one of your roses along. I want ALL the girls that see you to be so jealous they can't see straight. I really do love you Alyssa." "And I love you Jarrod."

He wrapped her up in a very loving embrace and gave her a very passionate kiss before going to dinner.

# Five

# Are Jack and Lynetta Through?

It was Monday morning, 6 a. m.  Rehearsal was just getting started. Adrianne was doing her warm up stretching. She looked at Leon out of the corner of her eye and looked quickly away when he saw her looking his way.

Leon moved over closer to her and said, "Hi ya cutie." and then winked at her.

All through rehearsal Leon and Adrianne kept throwing flirtatious looks at each other and doing little touches when they were near each other.

Finally, rehearsal was over. It was time to go home. Leon gave Jack a high five along with a loud "ALRIGHT!" He went over to Adrianne, "Hey Adrianne, can I see you later?" "As in a date?" "Well, yeah." "Sure, what time?" "How about I pick you up at 6:00?" "That will be fine. See you later."

Lynetta came over to Adrianne- "Adrianne, what's going on with you and Leon?" "He asked me to go out tonight." "Well, what did you say?" "I said yes. He's picking me up at 6:00. Why do I feel so nervous and excited. I mean it's not like we've never been out together before." "No, but I don't think this is a group date. It sounds like Leon wants to be *alone* with you this time." "OO that will be nice. I wonder what he has planned? Are you and Jack going out again?" "I don't know. Sometimes he asks me, you know, on the spur of the moment."

"Girl, that man takes you entirely too much for granted. The next time he asks you at the last minute you should tell him you're sorry, but you have other plans. Then watch his reaction."

"You know Dre, you're right. If he asks me tonight I'm going to be busy. Now you have fun tonight." "You too, whatever you're doing." "You know tonight I think I'll have a hot bubble bath and curl up with a good book and a good cup of hot herbal tea." "Oh, that sounds so good. I almost wish I could do that too. Oh well there's always tomorrow night. I'd better get home now. See you tomorrow." "Okay. And tell me tomorrow all about your date with Leon. Bye."

Jack said to Leon,"so dude, you want to go shoot some hoops tonight?" "Oh man, I can't. I asked Adrianne out on a date. How about tomorrow?" "Okay, tomorrow. 4:30?" "Hoops, 4:30, tomorrow, right. Later dude."

Later that night at home Jack was busy channel surfing- "Man, nothing, 500+ channels and nothing to watch. I wonder if Lynetta's busy?" Lynetta's phone rang while she was in the tub relaxing. Her phone was turned down low so she didn't hear it. Jack thought, "She must have stepped out and will be back soon," so he hung up.

After her bath Lynetta got out, dried off and put on something comfy. She went to the kitchen to make some tea. While she was waiting she stepped out onto the deck. Jack called back but she didn't hear the phone again.

Her tea kettle whistled so she went in to make her tea. She got her book and her tea and just before she settled down, her phone rang, again. She hurried over to answer it- "Hello?"

"Lynetta, is everything alright?" He asked in a worried tone. "Of course. Why wouldn't it be?" "Well, this is the third time I've called tonight and when you didn't answer...well, I was beginning to worry. You're sure you're alright? I can be there in a flash if you need anything." "No. I'm fine. Did you,..want something Jack?" "Well I just thought if you weren't busy tonight, we could go out. Want to? I can come over and get you." "Oh I'm sorry Jack, I just got out of a hot, tub and well, I have other plans tonight. But thanks for calling. It was sweet of you. Goodnight." She hung up quickly. "Lynetta? (dial tone) What?"

After she hung up on him he pulled the phone away and looked at the receiver very puzzled, wondering what just happened?

Lynetta settled on the couch and began to read her book while sipping her herbal tea. Soon she began to get sleepy and went to bed a little early. Meanwhile Jack kept going over, what happened on the phone, in his head. He couldn't figure it out so he finally went to bed.

Next morning he got up but he was so tired. He tossed and turned all night. Even the shower he took didn't help. He got to rehearsal and Leon saw him. "Dude, You look awful. What happened to you? Are you sick or something?" "No, I just didn't sleep well last night."

"I did! I had a fantastic time with Adrianne last night. She is sooo much fun. I can't believe I took so long to ask her out, I mean just the two of us. Jack, are you sure you're okay?" "Yeah Dude, I just need some O. J. I'll be fine. Don't worry. Hey seen Lynetta?"

"No, not yet." Just then Lynetta and Adrianne walked in. Jack looked over at Lynetta and nodded to her. She responded with a nod and a smile and continued talking with Adrianne.

Lynetta and Adrianne both shared with each other how each of their evenings went. The guys came over while Lyn and Dre were talking. Not really meaning to eavesdrop Jack overheard part of the conversation.

Then Danny called everyone over for stretching and warm-ups. After everyone was ready, they went through their daily routine and such. Jack found it extremely hard to concentrate ever since he overheard Lynetta talking to Adrianne.

Finally, rehearsal was over for the day. Lynetta said I really *need* a hot bath today. Danny *really* worked us hard today. I'll see you tomorrow Adrianne." She went home and never spoke to Jack or Leon.

Jack asked, "Where's Lynetta?" "I don't know man I never saw her after rehearsal. Let's ask Adrianne?

ADRIANNE!" "Hi Leon. Thanks again for a wonderful time last night!" "You're Welcome! It was fun. We'll have to do it again, soon. Say, where's Lynetta?" "Oh she went home already. Why?" "Is she mad at Jack for something or what?" "No, I don't think so. What's up?" "She's hardly talked to him since yesterday morning. Is she seeing another guy maybe?" "What? What *other* guy?" "Well who is Mark?" "Mark? Oh-h, Mark. No one." "What do you mean 'no one'? Does that mean he doesn't mean much to her or what?" "No silly I mean there is No *Mark* period." "Come on, Jack heard you two talking about him this morning right before rehearsal started. Can you deny that?" "No. You don't understand. There is no person Mark!" "Then what *were* you two talking about?" "A book Lynetta's been reading. The character's name is Mark and she was telling me how much (Mark) reminds her of Jack. She was also telling me what happens in the book. So there is absolutely *no one named Mark!*"

"So, why is she suddenly ignoring Jack?" "She's not." "She's not huh? Last night he called her 3 times. On the 3rd time she decided to answer but she was real short with him and then she hung up on him. Then this morning she hardly even said hi to him and ducked out right after rehearsal. That says to me that she's avoiding him." "Not that it's *any* of your business but just to show you how wrong you both are. I'll tell you all about last night and why she left so quickly today." And she did.

Leon said, "Oh wow. I need to talk to Jack. He's so sure she's seeing someone else that he doesn't know what to do." Leon looked around for Jack. Then he saw Brian. "Hey Brian have you seen Jack?"

"Yeah. He's really down. What happened? Did he and Lynetta have a fight?" "No. Just a huge misunderstanding. Do you know where he is now?" "I think he went home. I just know he left."

"Brian, if you see him, tell him, he HAS to call me immediately." "Okay, IF I see him." "Thanks Brian."

Leon went to Jack's apartment. No luck. He started looking everywhere he could think of. Finally he went to Lynetta's house. (knock, knock, knock). Lynetta answered in her robe. "Hi Leon. Sorry Jack's not here and I'm kind of busy. Can we talk later?" A guy's voice inside said, "Who is it Netta?" She said back, "Oh it's just a friend I'll be right there." Leon asked, "Who's that?" "Just a friend, uh, my cousin actually. Leon, I'm sorry I've gotta go now. Bye." She closed the door rather quickly.

Leon didn't know what to think. Suddenly he remembered the park they were at the other day and wondered if Jack might be there now?"

He went to check it out. There was Jack sitting on a swing. Leon went over to him. "Man, I've been looking all over for you. You okay dude?" Jack was staring at the ground. "I've lost her dude. I don't even know what I did but I've lost her. I messed up and now she's with someone else. How can I go on without the girl of my dreams and my heart? Nothing matters anymore. Nothing makes any sense. And I really don't care about anything any more. All I can see is her face, everywhere I go."

"I know man. It hurts, deep. But you have to go on. Don't give in. The pain will go away and you'll find someone else, eventually." " But I still love *her*. I can't just stop these feelings like turning off a switch." "I'm here for you man." "Leon, I think you should go. I don't want to get you down too." "Hey, I know let's go shoot some hoops or play a little one-on-one. You know B-ball always makes you feel better. Gets your mind off your troubles." "Not today. Thanks any way."

Over at Lynetta's her phone began to ring- "Shall I get that L?" "Get what?" "Your phone, it's ringing." "Oh yeah, thanks." Her guest answered (with a deep voice) "Lynetta 's, who's calling?" Adrianne said in a stunned voice, "Uh, H-Hello? Is Lynetta there?" "Yeah, just a minute...Lynetta phone for you. I think it's one of your girlfriends." "Thanks- Hello?"

"Girl, WHO IS THAT? I see now why you wanted to get home so fast." "Huh? No! No! Mark's my cousin." "Right, your *cousin*. That's a good one." "No, he *really is* my cousin. He came into town to surprise me and he's leaving tomorrow. I haven't seen him in a long time. The last time was I think a couple of years ago at a family reunion."

"You're not kidding?" "No, why?" "Just tell me this, how do you feel about Jack?" "Jack? You know that. I love him. Why?" "But how? Like a boyfriend or more like a brother?" "Okay, what's going on? You're acting very strange, so spill it." "Let's just say if you still love Jack you need to talk to him and pretty quick." "Why?" Lyn said in a concerned voice. "I'm not sure, but he may think you're seeing someone else." "But I'm not. How could he think that?"

"Think about it. You haven't said much to Jack in 2 days, you have a strange man in your house, at least he's a stranger to us and Jack overheard you mention 'Mark' from your book; Add it all up, in Jack's head? He is a guy." Lynetta got a shocked look on her face. "Oh Adrianne, I have to call him. I hope you're wrong! But if you're right..., Adrianne, I'll call you later. Bye." "Okay good luck, bye." Lynetta called

Jack but there was no answer. She called Brian, "No, sorry they're not here Lyn, but I'll tell them you called if I hear from either of them. Bye." "Thanks Brian"

"Mark I have to go out for a bit. I'll be back as soon as I can." Mark said, "Okay. Want me to wait up?" "No, you go ahead and go to bed when you want to. You have quite a drive tomorrow. Sorry I can't stay. I'm glad you came by to see me. Goodnight cuz. I had a wonderful time." Lynetta got dressed and went to look for Jack.

Meanwhile, Leon had convinced Jack to go home with him. Lynetta looked everywhere but still no Jack. Finally she went to Leon's place, knock knock. Leon answered the door, "What are *you* doing here?" "I've been looking everywhere for Jack and I can't find him. Have you seen him? (she sounded worried). "Yes, he's here."

"Thank goodness. Can I see him please?" "No!" "What? Why not?" "Haven't you done enough?" "What do you mean?" "He's my best friend and I won't let you hurt him any more. So, go back to Mark or whatever his name is..." "Mark? What does my cousin have to do with this?" "Oh, right, your *cousin*. You couldn't come up with something more original?" "Mark is my cousin. Why don't you believe me?" "Probably because of the way you've treated Jack for the last two days, that's why." "Leon, I can explain everything, if you'll just let me see him. It's all a huge misunderstanding, believe me." "I don't know. I'm more concerned about Jack's feelings. He's very hurt and confused right now and I don't want you to make it worse." "But if you'd just let me talk to him I can fix that. Leon, you can't keep me away from him forever. If you won't let me in to see him I'll just wait until you're not around him. But just remember, when I do get to see him and explain things, it was you who prolonged his pain and suffering when I wanted to end it quickly." "Okay, since you put it that way, you can come in and see him, but I'm going to be listening to everything you tell him." "Fine. Let's go."

Lynetta went in and found Jack sitting in a chair starring off into space, very depressed.

"Jack?" He slowly turned toward her voice and looked away again thinking she was only in his imagination. He really believed he'd lost her. She quickly went over to him, put her arms around him and said, "Jack, Jack, I'm so sorry. It's not what you think at all. Mark is my cousin not a boyfriend. He showed up at my house to pay me a surprise visit.

We haven't seen each other in years and he's leaving early tomorrow morning. I was looking all over for you but I couldn't find you. I had to leave right after rehearsal today because I was so sore I could hardly move. I just wanted to soak in a hot tub. And as for last night, I felt like you were taking me for granted, so I wanted some time alone to think about us and our relationship. But it didn't take me long to realize just how much I love you." She tried as hard as she could not to cry.

Jack looked up at her with tears in his eyes. He tried to speak but the words wouldn't come. The more he tried to the harder it became. Finally a tear spilled over and rolled down his cheek. Lynetta couldn't take it any more. She had hurt the man she loves. She cried out, "I'm so sorry Jack! I do still love you, I guess I always will, even if you don't love me any more. I can't really blame you."

She turned to hide her tears and leave. Jack managed, with a ragged voice to say, "Don't.Go.Please?!" Lynetta turned back around to see Jack reaching out for her. "Come to me. I-I love you." "Are you sure?" "I guess I <u>have</u> taken you for granted. I'm sorry. Forgive me? Please stay! I really do want you in my life. You are my life."

Lynetta rushed to his arms and he kissed her passionately, over and over again. At the same time she kissed him back and then he locked her in a loving embrace and whispered in her ear, "I'm never gonna let you go, NEVER!" Leon peeked around the corner. As he saw Jack and Lynetta together again he thought to himself, Yes, ALRIGHT, together again at last!

# Six

# Who Will Adrianne Choose?

Rehearsal was over for the day and over in the corner Jack and Leon were going over some of the new dance steps they learned. The girls came over to watch and then they joined in and all together Jack, Leon, Brian, Lynetta, Adrianne and Alyssa were rehearsing the new steps.

Danny saw them and came over, "Is there a problem I can help with?" Jack said, "Uh, no, Danny. We're just going over the new steps, they're pretty cool and we were just having some fun." "You kids just can't get enough? I would've thought you'd all be exhausted and going home."

Leon said, "Jack was just helping me with a part I keep messing up but I've got it now." Adrianne said, "We looked over and they looked like they were having fun so we thought we'd join in."

Danny said, "Well I'm glad you all like the new choreography. Now get out of here. You're done for today." Jack said, "But Danny, you make the work so much fun it doesn't seem like we're working."

Everyone agreed with Jack. "Well thank you, in any case you kids go home now. I'll see you tomorrow. If anyone needs help we'll work on it- TOMORROW!" Everyone said, "Okay, Danny, bye" "Goodbye."

Jack said, "Wow, that was so much fun!" Leon said, "Hey, I've got an idea. Who wants to come over to my place? We can do some dancing, work on the new steps, just hang out or whatever. I bought a ton of fresh fruit and sodas yesterday, what do you all say?" Everyone happily said yes.

Jack said, "Hey Lynetta, do you want to drop your car at your house and ride over with me?" "Thanks, that would be great."

Leon said, "Hey Adrianne, of you want me to, I can follow you to your place and you can ride over with me?" "Okay. Thanks Leon." "Hey Jarrod, we're all going over to my place for some fun. Alyssa's coming, how about you, do you wanna come?" "No thanks Leon. I'm really bushed. But you all have a great time. I'll see you tomorrow." "Okay, but if you change your mind just come on over. See ya."

Jack picked up Lynetta and Leon picked up Adrianne and they all met at Leon's apartment. Inside Lynetta and Dre started getting the food and drinks ready in the kitchen while Jack and Leon were setting up the music and moving furniture back to make room for dancing. "Thanks a lot Jack. I couldn't have done it all myself." "No sweat dude. Glad I could help. You girls need any help?"

Lynetta said, "Well, since you offered, here, taste this." She fed Jack a piece of fruit, then he, in turn, fed her a piece.

He said, "Mm-mm that's sooo good." Then she fed him one more piece. "Is that all I get?" "For now." "Can I have a kiss?" "H mm, well, maybe a little one." So she gave him a kiss.

Leon said, "Adrianne, can you come here for a minute?" "Okay Leon, I'll be right there. What is it?" "How are you with the new steps at rehearsal?" "Why? Are you having some trouble?" "A little, just this part right here..." He showed Adrianne the part he had down. Then he showed her where he was messing up. So she showed him the right way step by step.

Then she said, "You know, I'm having a little trouble with the next part. Every time I think I have it right to here, I'm always on the wrong foot and I can't figure out what I'm doing wrong." "Well, let me watch you and I'll see if I can spot what you're doing and we'll fix it." Leon put on some music. "Okay babe, show me what you know, ready, and 1,2,-1,2,3,4."

Adrianne went through the steps and still did it wrong. "Okay, lets do it together and you'll get it, I promise." They ran through it together and she still didn't get it right. While they were working on the routine the rest of the group showed up. Leon and Adrianne greeted everyone. The music was still playing and everyone said, "Alright, lets dance." Leon and Adrianne continued practicing and before long everyone was doing it with them. Adrianne then came to the part she was struggling with and stepped on Alyssa's foot. "Ouch!" "Oh, I'm so sorry Lyssa it's my fault. I just can't seem to get that part."

Adrianne started to get really upset. "I should just let my understudy take my place for this number. I just can't get it." Alyssa told her, "Honey, before this night's over you *will* have these steps down right, I promise even if we have to spend half the night doing it. But it isn't going to take that long because we're all going to help, right gang?" Everyone said, "RIGHT!" Adrianne said, "Thanks, you guys you're the best."

So they all danced, ate and drank the night away. Suddenly Lynetta said, "Okay, lets do it ." They all lined up across the floor and someone started the music. They did the entire routine to the end and Adrianne shouted, "I did it, I did it and I didn't mess up. Thank you all so much. You're so wonderful." Alyssa said, "I told you that you'd have it down before the night's over. You just needed to relax a little." "I guess so. Thanks Lyssa."

It was late, so they each said their goodbyes and headed on home. Jack took Lynetta and Leon took Adrianne home. Leon and Adrianne sat in the car talking then Adrianne turned and looked up into Leon's beautiful brown eyes. The conversation became lost as they both stared deep into each others eyes. Then, slowly, Leon leaned down and gently kissed her. "I'd... better get you inside so you can get some sleep." So Leon escorted Adrianne to her door and kissed her goodnight. "See you tomorrow babe." he said with a wink. "Goodnight Leon and thanks for a wonderful evening." "You're welcome and thank you." Leon kissed her once more then he went home with a smile on his face.

The next day after rehearsal Leon said to Adrianne, "I had a great time last night." "Me too." He took her hand in his and asked, "Can we get together tonight?" "I'd like that." she said as she smiled at him. "I'll pick you up at 6:00 for dinner, okay?" "I'll be waiting." He kissed her cheek. "See you soon."

At 6:00 Leon arrived at Adrianne's door. When she opened the door he thought, "She's beautiful!" Leon presented her with a bouquet of roses. "They're beautiful." "Not half as beautiful as you are." She went in to put them in water, then they went to dinner.

After dinner they went dancing. Once, while at the table, Leon excused himself for a bit and Adrianne was sitting alone. A guy walked up and said, "May I have this dance?" She politely said, "I'm sorry, but, no. My date will be back any moment. Thank you any way." "My loss, he's a lucky man." Just then Leon returned. "Who was that?" "Just someone asking me to dance." "You're so beautiful I knew someone would come over as soon as I was gone, so I hurried to get back." "Leon, you don't have to worry. I'm with you. I'm *your* date." "I know but tonight you're so beautiful." She blushed "Leon." "Well, you are! Would you like to dance?" "Not just now. I'd like to just sit here with you and talk or not talk. I just like being with you, having you near me."

"Me too. I can't take my eyes off of you, you're so beautiful. Your eyes they just sparkle. I could just sit and look at you all night." "I know what you mean. I feel that way about you too. I just don't want this night to end. I wish it would go on forever." "So do I. I've never felt like this before, with any girl." He reached across the table and took her hands in his. Just then a slow song began to play. "May I have this dance?" "Yes, you certainly may."

He lead her to the dance floor and they danced, almost as if they were one. As the music ended they looked deep into each others eyes and then they kissed. As they walked off the dance floor Leon was dieing to tell her how he felt about her but he thought it was too soon.

"I'd better take you home. It's getting late and we have an early start in the morning. Can't have a couple of sleepyheads at rehearsal." "You're right. And Danny wouldn't be very happy." "No. You're right about that. So let's go." Leon took Adrianne home. At her door he said, "I had a fantastic time. I hope you did too?" "I did. It was wonderful. Thank you. See you tomorrow. Goodnight Leon." "Goodnight Adrianne."

The next morning Jack noticed something very different about Leon. "Hey dude, what's up?" "Nothing." Jack had a look that said, yeah right. He wasn't buying it.

"Dude, this is me, come on, talk to me. I'm your best friend. How'd it go last night with Adrianne?"

"Dude, it was awesome. I got her a dozen red roses and when she opened the door I couldn't believe my eyes. I mean she was so beautiful I almost forgot the flowers were in my hand. Man, she took my breath away." "Whoa, are we talking about the same Adrianne? The same girl we rehearse with in sweats and a tee shirt?" "I know. She blew me away, completely. I only hope I didn't come off looking like a fool in front of her." "I'm sure you played it cool, right? You're used to working under pressure." Leon told Jack all about his date with Adrianne.

"Man, I so wanted to tell her how I felt, but I think it's a little too soon. So I just told her what a fantastic time I had." "What did she say?" "She said pretty much the same thing."

Jack felt like Leon wasn't telling him everything. So he said, "And... what else?" Leon said, "What?" "Oh, come on man, I know you, spill it." "Okay, she said she didn't want the night to end and wished it would go on forever." "Whoa dude, she's got it bad for you." "Yeah? But I still wonder if I should have told her how I felt." "Leon, if she said *that*, don't worry. Just take it slow and let it happen the way it should. Everything will work out. Just enjoy being together." "I know you're right. But it's hard to not run up to her and say...well, you know." " I know. So let's go shoot hoops after rehearsal and get your mind off of this for awhile." "Okay, good idea. Later."

Adrianne walked in and Lynetta went over to her. "Adrianne? What is with you this morning? You're absolutely glowing. What happened?"

Adrianne told Lynetta excitedly, "Leon took me out on a date last night. Oh Lynetta, we had the best time. He brought me a dozen red roses, took me to dinner and dancing. I never wanted it to end. My heart was pounding so hard I was sure everyone in the room could hear it. The way he made me feel, I've never, ever felt that way before. It was incredible. The way he looked at me just made my heart melt. There were a couple of times I could hardly breathe. And dancing with him, especially to a slow song, oh Lynetta, I was beginning to wonder if it was real or a dream."

"Well I can certainly tell he makes you <u>very</u> happy. You haven't stopped smiling since you came in here and I can feel the energy pouring out of you right now, just as you stand there." "I only hope I didn't make a fool of myself. The way I was feeling, it didn't feel like me." "I'm sure you kept your cool. Remember you're used to working under pressure." "But this is different." "Look, let's go shopping after rehearsal and take your mind off last night for awhile, okay?" "Okay, but it won't help." "We'll see."

After rehearsal Leon went over to Adrianne with Jack close behind. At the same time Lynetta was right behind Adrianne. "Hi Adrianne. It's nice to see you again." "Hi Leon. It's nice to see you again." "Jack and I are going to shoot some hoops for awhile." "Oh that's great. Lynetta and I are going shopping at the mall. So I guess I'll see you, later." "Yeah, see you... later." Leon went over to her and gave her a goodbye kiss. "Bye doll." "Goodbye Leon."

Jack and Lynetta looked at each other in disbelief. It appears that their best friends like each other, a lot! So Jack kissed Lynetta goodbye and the guys went off and spent their time shooting hoops awhile.

The girls went shopping at the mall. Lynetta saw a beautiful dress and went in to check it out. Adrianne went over to look at the blouses. Suddenly a good looking young man came up behind Adrianne and said, "Adrianne? Is that you?" She turned around quickly and said, "Ricky?" and gave him a great big hug. Just then Lynetta came over and was surprised to see her best friend in the arms of another guy, but didn't say anything. Adrianne introduced him to Lynetta. "Lynetta this is Ricky. We've known each other what, forever it seems."

Adrianne talked to Ricky about meeting tomorrow for lunch. Lynetta didn't quite know what to think or say. All she could think was, (what about Leon?) Lynetta turned back just in time to hear Adrianne say, "Okay, it's a lunch date, tomorrow at noon?" "It's great to see you again. I can't wait to catch up with you, Dre. See you tomorrow." Lynetta and Adrianne finished their shopping and Lynetta took Adrianne back to her car but they didn't talk much. Lynetta didn't quite know what to say to her friend.

"See you later Lynetta. Thanks for the shopping trip it was fun." "Bye Adrianne. See you later." Both girls headed for home.

Next morning. It was Saturday. Adrianne got up and started to make coffee when suddenly the phone rang. She answered it, "Hello?" "Hi gorgeous." She asked, "Who is this?" "It's Ricky." "Oh Hi. Hey, how'd you get my number, it's unlisted?" "I called your mom and she gave it to me." "It figures." "I was glad she was still at that number and that she remembered me. She was more than happy to give me your number. I hope you don't mind." "No. I was just surprised is all." "Are we still on for lunch? I know you're a busy lady these days so I thought I should check." "Sure, do you want to meet somewhere or what?" "Well, if you'll tell me where you live and how to get there I'll pick you up." "Okay."

She gave Ricky the address and directions and then got ready for her lunch date. By the time he arrived she was ready to go. Knock Knock She opened the door. "Hi Ricky." "Hi there beautiful." He pulled from behind his back a single red rose and gave it to her with a kiss. "What's this for?" "A beautiful rose for a beautiful lady." "Oh Ricky you shouldn't have. It's beautiful. Thank you. I'd better put it in water then we can go. Okay, I'm ready. Let's go."

"Where would you like to eat milady? Your choice. Just name it." "Oh I don't care really, anywhere is fine with me." They went out to his car. "Oh wow! Is this your car?" "Yeah, this is my baby. She's a sweet little machine and purrs like a kitten under the hood." "I love the 1968 Mustang. That's what I call style in a car." "Well she's your chariot today babe. She'll take you anywhere you want to go." "Okay." She told Ricky their destination and how to get there and off they went.

Meanwhile at Leon's apartment, Leon woke up and thought to himself, "H mm, Saturday morning I wonder if Adrianne is up yet? Think I'll call and find out." Adrianne's phone rang but no answer. Maybe she went out for a jog. I'll call a little later."

Leon called Jack, "Hey dude, wanna go get some coffee? I'm buying." "Sure, where at?" "I'll just swing by and get you." "Okay, see ya soon." Leon picked up Jack and the guys went to a nearby coffee shop. They were just talking "guy talk" when they pulled up to the Coffee Cafe. Leon stopped in mid-sentence when he looked up and saw Adrianne sitting in the Cafe with another guy. Jack looked up and saw them too. He said to Leon, "Dude maybe it's not what it looks like. You said she told you she had a wonderful time with you, right?" "Yeah, but look how closely they're sitting together."

Just then Ricky reached over and put his hand on hers and they were laughing. Then he took both of her hands in his and brought them to his lips and kissed them. Jack said, "Let's go find out what's going on and who the guy is." "No man. It's obvious she's seeing someone else. I was just a one-night-stand. Look how happy she is with him." "I still say we should go find out who he is and what she's doing with him."

"No. She's old enough to know who she wants to go out with. It's not like we've been dating for a long time, even though it was a dream I had. She's made her choice. I'm done. Let's get out of here."

"Okay for now, but Leon, I think you're making a huge mistake." Leon dropped Jack off at home and said, "Promise me you won't tell <u>anyone</u> what we just saw, especially Adrianne or Lynetta. Promise?" "Okay, I promise. I'll see you later dude." "Okay, later." Jack went in and Leon took off.

Ricky took Adrianne to the park and they went for a walk. While they were walking they were reminiscing about the days gone by when they were both younger." Ricky told her, "I have a secret I never told anybody. Not even you, until now." "What?" "Remember all the times we got really close to a kiss and someone would always interrupt?" "Yeah." "Well this time I'm not going to let anything interrupt us. I always wanted to do this." Ricky leaned over and gently kissed her lips. Adrianne was lost in the moment. But just as Ricky was about to kiss her again she came to her senses and pulled away from him. Surprised by her reaction he asked, "Dre, what is it?"

"Ricky, we've known each other since we could walk. We're very good or even best friends." "I know. That's what makes it so perfect. So what's the problem?" "The problem is you assume that I feel the same as you do. You never even asked if there was anyone special in my life." "Well you never told me there was anyone and I don't see a ring on your finger. So, *is* there someone else? And by the way you *did* kiss me back you know." "I know. That was a mistake." (She was disappointed in herself.)

"Was it? I think you wanted me to kiss you as much as I wanted to." "Maybe, no, I don't know. I'm so confused right now. There is a guy and I'm not sure if we're just friends or if there's something more. Leon and I have been out as friends lots of times. But the other night we went on a date, just us two and I saw him in a whole new way and I liked it." "And you want to pursue it further." "I also don't want to take a chance on destroying a very special friendship that we've always had."

"Did I spoil it when I kissed you?" "I don't think so. I think somewhere deep inside you and me there was a little boy and a little girl who always wanted to kiss each other but were always denied, until now. But Ricky, we aren't that little boy and girl anymore. We are, however, very good friends and I hope we always will be. I'm sorry if I hurt you or led you on. Can you forgive me?" "There's nothing to forgive. I think you're right. We were acting out a fantasy we've both had for years and now it's gone. My dream of kissing you came true and now I'm okay. So, when do I get to meet this Romeo that's swept my best friend off her feet?"

Dre smiled and said, "How about tomorrow afternoon?" "How about I take the two of you to lunch tomorrow? My treat." "Are you sure?" "Yeah and you can invite some of your other friends you were telling me about, like Jack, Lynetta, Lyssa, Jerrod and Brian." "That will cost way too much." "Okay how about, you and Leon and two of the others?" "Jack and Lynetta are Leon's and my best friends." "Okay invite them." "Okay, if you're absolutely sure?" "Yes, I'm absolutely sure. Now call them."

Adrianne called Leon, (it rang but no one answered) "He's probably shooting hoops at Jack's place." So she called Jack, "Yo, talk to me." "Jack, it's Adrianne, is Leon over there? He doesn't seem to be home. (he didn't answer, he was thinking of what to say to her.) Jack are you still there?" "Yeah, I'm here." "Well, do you know where Leon is?" "I didn't know you cared." "What? Just what is that supposed to mean?" "You have to ask Leon. I promised I wouldn't say anything to you." Rather annoyed Adrianne said, "Well I can't reach Leon so you'll HAVE to tell me. What happened?" Sarcastically-he said, "Where's your new boyfriend?" "My what? What new boyfriend? You mean Leon? I don't know. Okay Jack, enough games. Tell me straight out. Where is Leon?" "I-don't -know." "Jack?" "Look, he dropped me off and I came inside and he left, that's all I know."

"Well I haven't talked to him in a couple of days." Sarcastically he said, "No kidding." "Now what's *that* supposed to mean?" "I'm surprised you even remember his name." "Okay Jack, now you're not making ANY sense at all." "Alright, I'll tell you, but I'm breaking a promise. Here it is, Saturday morning Leon picked me up and we went down to the coffee shop near by." "You mean just down the street?" "Yeah." "Wow I was there Saturday morning and I didn't see you. Why didn't you say Hi?" "Because you were too busy holding hands with your new boyfriend." "My new boy...oh no! You must mean Ricky." "Oh is that his name?" "No, Jack, you have it all wrong." "What, you weren't holding hands?" "No I mean he's not my boyfriend. He's just a friend."

"I have lots of friends but we don't hold hands like that." "But Ricky and I have known each other since we could walk. That's most of my life." "So what about Leon, how and where does he fit in?" "How does he *fit in*?" "He's crazy about you. Oh NO. Don't tell him I told you that. I wasn't supposed to say anything, and I promised." "Why? Because of Ricky? There's nothing going on between me and Ricky. We are JUST old friends. Please Jack I can't lose Leon. If he really does like me, I need your help. He has to see that he is the only guy in my heart. Will you help me?" "I might, if you tell me everything up front. I might believe you."

"Alright, I'll tell you most of it. But I'll tell Leon everything but not over the phone. I'll be right over."

Adrianne went over to Jack's place. Jack was able to get Leon on the phone with a special code they have. "Hey Leon, how are you doing man?" "Hangin' in there. What's up?" "I have some good news for you." "Great, I could use a little about now. What is it?" "Well, I'll tell you when I get there I'm coming over. See you soon." "Okay, see ya."

Adrianne pulled up as Jack was coming out. "Now that's timing Dre. Get in and let's go." "Where are we going?" "Just get in. You'll see." Jack drove Adrianne over to Leon's place, explaining his plan as they went. When they got to the door Adrianne stayed out of sight so Leon couldn't see her when he opened the door. Jack knocked. "Hey dude, it's me, Jack." Leon came to the door, "Hey Jack, come on in." Jack went in and motioned to Adrianne to sneak in behind him. Adrianne slipped in and into another room without Leon seeing her. "So, Jack, what's the good news you couldn't tell me on the phone?" "Well I found out who the mystery man is." Sarcastically- "Oh. Great just what I wanted to hear about."

Just then Adrianne stepped in and quietly said, "But you need to hear the truth Leon and I'm going to stay here and tell you until you hear it, no matter how long it takes!" Stunned by the sound of Adrianne's voice Leon sat up quickly. "What are you doing here? (Sarcastically)- Shouldn't you be with your new boyfriend?" "I thought that was you Leon." "Me? I'm not the one who was...holding your hands Saturday morning over coffee or whatever. You sure did look cozy to me." "Well if you saw me why didn't you come over and say hi, or something?" "And say what exactly? It was clear to me who you wanted to be with!"

"Then you need glasses, and an education. The education is what I'm here to give you, so listen up!"

Jack was sure Adrianne had things well under control. So while they were deep in conversation he sneaked out and went home.

"Ricky just happens to be my oldest and dearest friend, Leon. We've known each other since both of us could walk. We're comfortable with each other, BUT, we don't have a romantic relationship. Oh, sure, we love each other but we're not in-love. He's more like a brother. Do you understand what I'm trying to say?" She went over and took hold of his hands   and looked straight into his eyes. "So, he really is JUST a friend?" "Yes Leon, he's just a friend. But you mean much more than that to me." "I do? Really?" "Yes, really! And Ricky wants to meet you so he wants to take us out to lunch, along with Jack and Lynetta, that is...unless we're through?"

"I'm sorry Adrianne. Jack was right. I should have come over to see you but I was so jealous and angry I decided to leave. He was also right about it not being what it looked like. Adrianne, can you ever forgive me?" "Leon, I already have."

"I guess there's no denying it now." "What?" "How much I really do love you and care for you." "You do?" "Yes." "Me too." "I wanted so much to tell you the other night but I was afraid of what your reaction would be and I didn't want to push you. I also thought it may be too soon to say it. But you know, it feels so good when I do, so, I love you Adrianne." "I love you Leon."

They hugged and kissed and Adrianne stayed awhile since Jack left and went home.

Authors note: All's well that ends well!- Or is it just the beginning...? What do you think?

# Seven

## (Part 1)
## Where is Jack?

Rehearsal was over and almost everyone was headed for home. Jack, Lynetta, Leon and Adrianne were the last ones to go.

Jack asked, "Hey guys, wanna hang out awhile?" Leon said, "Yeah, that would be cool." The girls both agreed. Lynetta suggested, "Let's go get some ice cream treats while we decide where we're going and what we're doing." Jack said, "Awesome idea. I am rather overheated." (Jack shot Lynetta a look with a hint of a smile and a wink that made Lynetta blush.)

Leon said, "Okay people, let's go get some ice cream." "Yea, hooray!" Everybody cheered. Jack said, "Let's all go in my car." Everybody piled into Jack's car and soon they were at the ice cream store.

Everyone got their ice cream and they went outside to eat it. Jack let Lynetta have some of his cone and suddenly he dabbed a little ice cream on the end of her nose. So she chased Jack around the parking lot. She was just about to pay him back when he grabbed her and kissed the ice cream away and then gave her a big huge kiss right there in the parking lot. Adrianne said, "Hey you two that's enough." "I know, let's all go to the park. It's not far."

They all agreed and headed to the park. They split up and played in the park awhile, the swings, the merry-go-round, the slide, all over the park.

Jack was looking around for Lynetta. He saw her across the park. "Oh there she is." Suddenly, out of nowhere it seemed, a handsome young man appeared right in front of Lynetta and kissed her on the lips. She seemed surprised but not shocked. She smiled at him and started talking to him. Jack didn't know what to think. "Maybe I should go talk to him and let him know just who he's messing with." But then, before he could even take a step, right before his eyes this guy was hugging *his* girl and she *didn't* seem to mind. Jack's heart sank. He couldn't bear to watch any more.

Leon saw the look on Jack's face. He said, "Dude what's wrong?" Jack shot a glance over to the guy with Lynetta. Leon looked in that direction and said, "Who's that?" "I don't know. But I'm out of here." He tossed his keys to Leon and said, "You can take my car home." Then he took off on foot.(Too upset to drive.) Leon called to Jack "Dude wait up. Come back. Don't do this."

But Jack kept walking, shaking his head. His anger and pain were growing. But he was more hurt than angry. "How could she do this to me after telling me how she felt about me?" He headed for home.

Lynetta saw Leon and Adrianne and headed in their direction. The young man disappeared when she turned away from him so Lynetta never saw him leave.

She caught up to Leon and Adrianne. "Hi guys. Where is Jack?" In a rather *cool* tone Leon said flatly, "Gone, what did you expect?" "What do you mean, gone? You're joking?" "No! He left after he saw you and..., Leon looked around but the guy was gone, hey, where'd he go?" "Where'd who go?" "Who? The kissing bandit that's who." Lyn turned around and was surprised that her friend was gone. She called out, "Ronny? Ronny, where are you?"

"You know this guy?" "Well sort of. I knew him when we were kids but he moved and I never saw him again until today. I had a crush on him back then (she said with a smile,) and I think he had one on me but his dad got transferred so that was the end of that." "Well that explains what we saw. I guess his feeling for you haven't changed over the years." "But *mine* <u>have</u> and I have Jack now and I love HIM. Ronny's just part of my past." "It looked to us like he wants to be part of your present and *maybe* your future."

"Well he's out of luck." "There may be one problem." "What?" "Jack saw you two together and it looked <u>real</u> to us." "Oh no..." Lynetta quickly called Jack on her cell phone but Jack had turned it off so she left him a message: "Jack, don't erase this before you listen to it. What you saw was not what it looked like. Please call me. I can explain. I love you, I really do. Call as soon as you listen to this message. Please!"

She turned to Jack's best friend, Leon, "Leon, his phone went right to voice mail. Now what do I do? Did he tell you where he was going at least?" "No, sorry, he didn't."

Jack was just walking to clear his head of what he saw. But it was no use. The harder he tried to forget the more it played over and over again in his memory. As he was walking he thought he was being followed. So he looked back a couple of times and noticed the same dark sedan with darkened windows going the same pace and direction he was. He tried to ignore it but when he realized it really was following him he wondered, "What should I do? Run, turn back, what?"

While he was deciding what to do the sedan pulled up alongside of him and the window rolled down. From inside, a woman's voice said, "Mr Zachry, would you like a ride somewhere?" He turned toward the car's open window thinking: "My instincts tell me I should just keep walking." He looked into the car trying to see a face but it was too dark inside. Then the voice said, "I'm a big fan of yours and you look worried. I'd like to help, if I may?" He thought of how soothing her voice sounded. But still, should he get into a strange car with a total stranger? Then he decided, "Why not?" He threw caution to the wind and said, "Thank you" and got in the car. She asked where he was headed and he said, "Nowhere really, just taking a walk."

She gave instructions to the driver and they took off. She engaged Jack in conversation during which she asked if he would help her choose a cologne fragrance for her boyfriend. "It's his birthday and I wanted to give him some new cologne but I can't decide which one to give him. They're both nice. So I thought I should get a guys opinion, would you please?" He smiled and said, "Sure." She handed him two bottles. The first one was nice, not too strong but the second one didn't smell like much, so she said to try it again. After he did he felt very strange and suddenly everything went black.

When he came to he discovered his worse nightmare. His hands and feet were tied, he was gagged and blindfolded, "Oh, No! I've been kidnapped." He heard muffled voices nearby. One sounded like the woman in the car, as near as he could tell. He heard a door open so he pretended to still be out but it was hard because he had a huge headache. He felt someone sit down beside him and begin to stroke his hair and his face. It was her. He could tell.

She softly said, "I'm gonna treat you so good you'll never want to leave me and you'll forget all about your little girlfriend and all the pain she's caused you." She began talking to someone else in the room, "Take the gag off *carefully.* He won't yell, not that it would do any good anyway, way out here. And he's not the type. But let me know if he gives you any trouble when he wakes up."

Jack thought to himself: "So that's it. Lynetta must have been set up to make me leave her. Well, we'll just see about that. I should have listened to Leon. But why did I get into that car? I know better than that. Don't worry Lynetta, I'll come back to you Baby, I promise! But first I have to get out of here, wherever here is."

Jack's friends were trying to figure out where he had gone. Leon said, "He must have gone home. Jack gave me his keys so I'll run over to his place and check." At Jack's place, nothing, no sign of him being there at all. Leon talked out loud as if Jack was really there, "Jack, dude where are you? Give me a sign." Leon went back to the park. "Sorry guys still no Jack. You?" "No." "Well, I'm gonna stay at his place because I don't think he realized his door key is on his car keyring."

Lynetta said, "I'm staying too. It's my fault he left in the first place." "Don't go there. Did you know some guy was going to just walk out of the bushes and plant a big kiss on your lips? I don't think so, I think *he* planned *it* and Jack's disappearance." "No one said Jack has disappeared." "Well what more proof do you need Lynetta?"

"Maybe he's just wandering around town." "Well in any case I'm going to be there if and when he comes home. Then we'll know for sure!" Lynetta and Adrianne both said, "Me too." Then Adrianne said, "We'll all wait together." They all got to Jack's apartment and tried not to think the worst but that was very hard to do.

By now, Jack's headache was really too much, so he pretended to be waking up with it. The woman was once again sitting beside Jack and said, "So you finally woke up. How do you feel Jack?" "My head is killing me." "Oh, that will wear off but I could give you something for the pain if you want sweetie." "That would be great." She spoke to someone else, "You there, go into the bathroom and bring Jack 2 aspirin and a glass of water. I'll be back in a little while." "Yes ma'am"- the other voice said.

He took the aspirin and soon his headache was gone. Maybe now he could think clearly and figure a way to get out of there and back to Lynetta. "Well it's obvious I'm being well guarded cause this same guy hasn't left the room. I can hear him breathing." Then *she* came back in, "How do you feel Jack, headache gone?" "Yeah, thanks. Can I take this blindfold off now?"

"Maybe a little later. I would love to see those gorgeous blue eyes again. But not just yet." She ran her fingers through his hair. "You have the most gorgeous hair I just love to run my fingers through it." Just as she touched his hair Jack pulled away thinking, "Lynetta's the ONLY ONE who can run her fingers through *my* hair lady."

"Now Jack, if you act like that it will take longer to get that blindfold off." "Sorry, I'm just not used to people touching my hair, except my hairdresser of course." "Oh well, if that's all it is?" Then Jack said to her,"You know, I sure would love to see the gorgeous face that goes with that sweet, awesome voice." "Oh Jack, how sweet. Well, if you're a good boy tonight I just may consider it tomorrow morning, okay?" "Okay. I'll be good. But do you think I could use the bathroom?" "Oh I'm sorry, sure you can. -take him in there, untie him and tie him back up afterwards. See you later baby." "Bye, thanks."

Back at Jack's place, Lyn said, "I'm really worried now. It's been dark for over an hour now and he's still not here. He hasn't called either. I think we should call the police." Leon said, "But the police can't do anything for 24 hours. And I would feel pretty dumb if we filled out a missing person report and Jack came walking in his own front door right after it was filed. No we have to wait."

"But this isn't like him Leon. He's always been in touch with one of us sometime during the day. Right?" Leon agreed. Dre said, "Well it can't hurt to ask a police officer and see if we should make a report." Lyn said, "I agree. I'll call. Hello, police? I have a friend who took off this afternoon extremely upset, on foot and left all his keys behind with us. He's turned his phone off so we can only leave a message on his phone. We're at his apartment and he hasn't returned. He hasn't tried to call any of us and that just isn't like him. Should we fill out a missing person report?" Officer: "What time did you last see him?" "About 5:00 or 5:15 this afternoon." "Well we can't really do anything officially for 24 hours and maybe he just stopped somewhere and lost track of the time. He may show up any minute. I'll tell you what, if you're this worried and he is a creature of habit, and he's not back by 2 p m tomorrow afternoon call back and ask for me, Sargent Shelby and I'll help you fill out a report, okay?" "Okay and thank you."

"You're welcome. But sweetie, I'm sure your boyfriend has had time to cool off and is on his way back to you as we speak." "My boyfriend? (surprised),but I never said..." "Sweetie, you didn't have to. I've been at this job a long time and had lots of calls like yours and you'd be surprised how many guys walked through the door either while I was still on the phone or just after I hung up. So keep a good thought and try not to worry okay?" "Okay. And thanks Sargent Shelby. I feel much better. I'm sure you're right." "Call me Lynn."

"Thanks Lynn and I'm Lynetta." "Okay, well Lynetta your boyfriend sounds like a pretty level headed guy so get some sleep and patch things up tomorrow, alright?" "Alright I will. You're terrific. Goodbye." "Goodbye Lynetta." They hung up.

Leon and Dre both looked at Lynetta and said, "Well?" Lyn said, "Well, nothing. I just overreacted. Jack is probably on his way home right now. He's a big boy who can take care of himself." Leon said, "Wow talk about an about-face, that was a complete 180. Hey, who are you and what did you do with Lynetta?" he smiled. "Funny. I'm still here. I just got some great advice. I know! Let's watch a movie. It will take our minds off things and Jack will probably walk in by the end of the movie if not before. Okay?" Leon and Dre both agreed. Leon said, "So, what do we watch?" "Let's see what Jack has."

As they began looking through the movies suddenly Lynetta said, "I've got one." Lynetta went over to put the movie in and Leon asked, "Which one?" "The Fox and The Hound", by Walt Disney".

Dre said, "Oh I love this movie." "Me too." Leon said. The girls both looked at Leon, then each other and Leon said, "What?" The girls both said, "Aw Leon." Leon said, "Just watch the movie."

The girls giggled and Dre said, " I didn't know Jack had this movie." Lynetta said, "I saw it one night when I was over here and I was looking for a movie for us to watch." The movie began and Lynetta thought to herself, "Jack, please come home soon. I miss you and I *do* love you."

Back over to Jack... "Hey dude. I know you're here to watch me but you know my back is getting sore from just laying here. You think I could at least sit up or something?" "Sorry man, I just do as the lady said. That's what I get paid for." "I know, but could you at least ask, for me, please?" "Okay. You seem like a good kid. I'll see what I can do." "Thanks man." "Sure, okay."

The woman came back in, "How's our guest doing?" "He's not feeling so good ma'am. He'd like to be allowed to sit up cause his back is getting sore. He hasn't tried to get away, or anything, and you can keep him tied up, only, let him-" "Okay, okay, just make him comfortable." She quickly left the room.

"Okay man, you got your wish. You get to sit up awhile." "Thanks dude." The guard untied Jack's hands so he could stretch and sit up by himself. "Oh, that feels much better." "Just, please don't try anything. I don't want to have to shoot you." "Don't worry. I just need to stretch right now. The last time I was flat on my back this long, I was in the hospital."

"Yeah, I dislocated my shoulder once when I got into it with some dude checkin' out <u>my</u> girl. So, how did you end up here with Syl...uh like this?"

"You mean you don't know who I am?" "All I know is your name is Jack something." "Zachry. Then you <u>don't</u> know who I am? Don't you ever go to a play or read the paper?" "Sure, I love Hagar the Horrible and that Dagwood comic. Sometimes I even read Family Circus." "Family Circus, that's nice." She quickly opened the door and walked in, "Hey, what's all the talking going on in here? I'm not paying you to make friends with him, just watch him. If you can't do that I'll get someone else. Got it?"

"Yes ma'am. Sorry, won't happen again." "I hope you're right. I don't want to break in a new one." She turned toward Jack, "And you, don't make me put the tape back on those gorgeous lips again." "No ma'am, sorry." "Alright then." "Excuse me, I don't want to be a bother but could I get like a sandwich or something, a pickle just something to make my stomach stop making noises?" "You haven't eaten yet?" "No ma'am. I don't usually eat till about 7:00." "I'll see what there is." She left.A little while later she came back. "Here give this to him, "I hope you like it. Goodnight."

After she left the last time, Jack whispered, "Sorry dude, didn't mean to get you in trouble earlier." "I'm cool. Here eat this then get some sleep. See you in the morning." Jack tried to go to sleep but he kept thinking about Lynetta, Leon and Adrianne and what they must be going through. "I wonder if they've called the police yet to report me as missing? (yawn) I guess I'll think about it tomorrow." Jack fell asleep.

Back at Jack's apartment, Leon and Dre were curled up on the couch together and Lyn was in the chair trying to cuddle a pillow. She kept looking over at the couch, wishing Jack was there to cuddle with. She didn't realize she was staring, then Leon caught her looking at them with a sad look on her face. "Hey, Lyn, come on over here. There's plenty of room. Don't sit there alone, come, sit with us." Surprised she was caught staring, her reply was, "Oh, no! I'm fine, I'm good right here, really." "I insist. Come on over here. It'll be more fun with the 3 of us." Dre looked over and said, "Please Lyn, come sit with us." They looked at her with "puppy dog eyes." "Okay, I can't ignore both of you." She sat down beside Leon and as he put his other arm around her he said, "I promised Jack, back when you two got serious, I'd always look out for you if he wasn't able to. So don't make me break that promise, okay?" "Okay, I didn't know. Thanks Leon. You're a great friend. You too Dre." "Anytime you need me, I mean that." Dre said, "That goes double for me."

The movie played on and soon Adrianne got up to get something. She looked over and saw that Leon had fallen asleep. She smiled, leaned over and kissed his cheek. She looked at Lynetta who was now crying. Dre said softly, "Is it Jack or the movie?" " I guess a little of both." "I'm sorry, maybe things will be better tomorrow. Want something from the kitchen?" "No thanks. I'm good." "Be right back."

Dre was gone for a bit. Leon began to snuggle up to Lynetta who was just trying to get comfortable. She said to Leon, "Hey wake up and go to bed." Leon stirred and while Lyn was looking at him he leaned over and kissed her just as Adrianne returned with a snack tray. "Well isn't this cozy?" Dre said, then gave Leon a sock in the arm. That woke him up. "What? The movie over?" "Is that all you can say? Movie over? Okay hot lips I think you need to go to bed." He sat up and looked at Lynetta who still had a shocked look on her face. Leon said, "What? Is it Jack?" Lyn shook her head, unable to speak. Dre broke in with, "You were kissing Lynetta." "What? No way. NO! I-I was kissing you." He pointed to Adrianne, standing with her arms crossed.

"But I was in the kitchen and my lips don't kiss long distance." "Then that means..., oh Lyn I-I'm so sorry. I never... oh man Jack is going to kill me. And after I promised to look out for you. He'll never trust me again." Totally embarrassed, Leon covered his face with his hand. Lynetta sat up and quickly said, "We won't tell him. He'll never know." Leon said, "Yes he will. He always knows when I'm lying." "We'll just explain where you were when you fell asleep and you thought you were kissing Adrianne. It will be okay. I promise." "Well it's late. We should all go to sleep and hope tomorrow is a much better day. Goodnight Leon, Adrianne." "Goodnight Lyn, again I'm sorry." Dre to Lynetta, "Goodnight sweetie. See you in the morning." They each found a place to lie down and went to sleep.

The next day Jack woke up still blind folded and tied up. The woman came in, "Good morning Jack. Are you awake yet?" "I guess so." "How would you like to shower and change *and* take that blindfold off?" "That sounds great." "Okay but first...", she leaned over and kissed him on the lips and she was sure he kissed her back, then she took the blindfold off. After his eyes had adjusted a bit he looked around the room, the window had bars on it, the only door was guarded probably 24/7 by a very capable looking guy, with a gun. Just then a woman came out of the bathroom.      "Everything 's ready. Untie him. Hello Jack I'm Sylvia. I took the liberty of buying you some new clothes. I hope you like them. Any way there's clean towels and soap for your shower. After you're dressed we'll see about your breakfast. See you later." She kissed him again and left.

Jack went into the bathroom, "No windows, except one tiny one big enough for a cat or small dog, and too high to reach, bummer. I should have figured. Oh well at least they'll let me have a shower." While he was in the shower he was thinking of Lynetta and Leon, hoping that they had called the police. He suddenly remembered a show he had watched with Leon called "Kidnapped", where a husband who'd been kidnapped connected with his wife by mental telepathy. "I've gotta try something. Now what was it he did?" He pictured Lynetta in his mind then thinking her pet name that only he calls her by, Baby L, he began to concentrate very hard, "Baby L, help me, please help me, I'm trapped. I Love You! I'm trying to come home to you. Call the police, Now!"

Back at Jack's apartment, Lyn woke up suddenly, calling out, "Jack I'm here! I'm here, I Love You too!" Suddenly Leon and Dre raced to her side. "What? What is it?" All Lynetta could say was, "Jack, in trouble, trapped, needs help. But where? Where are you?" Lynetta started to cry. "We have to call the police." Dre said, "Honey we're going to at 2:00 this afternoon remember?" "No. Now! We have to call now! Later maybe too late." " Honey, you're just upset. We all are. You're emotionally spent. You need to calm down. Look, there's nothing here for breakfast so we'll all go out for breakfast and things will look differently. You probably just had a nightmare you were waking up from."

Leon came out and said, "Did I hear someone mention breakfast? Let's go I'm starved." They went down to the corner "Coffee Shoppe" and got breakfast. While they were waiting for their food the same guy that caused Jack to leave just walked in the door. "Lynetta? Is that you?" She turned around, "Ronny! Where did you go yesterday?" "Oh I had to be somewhere and I was running late, sorry I couldn't say goodbye. It's lucky we ran into each other again."

Leon and Dre look at each other with the same thought, "Yeah, some coincidence. I bet he's been following her."   Lynetta said, "Well let me introduce you to two of my best friends, Leon and Adrianne. Guys this is my old friend Ronny. I met Ronny in 2nd grade and we hit it off. We were best friends from the start. He was the closest thing I had to a boyfriend, back then, till he moved away." "Oh come on Netta, they don't want to hear all that. We *were* best friends though. I miss that. I never could replace you. You're a tough act to follow." "Oh Ronny." (she blushed.)

Leon asked, "So how did you get so lucky yesterday?" "I saw her interview on Extra about local talent and started making calls. Then I wondered if her mom still lived in the same house or at least had the same number that I still have. So I called and she remembered me. I told her I was down here and wanted to see Netta but didn't know how to reach her, so she gave me her cell phone number. She told me Lynetta is very hard to reach during the day so while I was waiting for evening to come I went to the park. I couldn't believe my eyes when I went into the park and there she was, right in front of me. All I could think of was kissing her. So I did."

Leon said, "I suppose you thought her boyfriend wouldn't mind you stealing a kiss from his girl?" "I never really thought about it. It all happened so fast." Lyn shot Leon a look that said "BACK OFF". Dre chimed in, with a more friendly tone, " So Ronny where are you staying while you're here?"

"Oh I'm staying with a friend who lives here. She always said I could stay with her if I was down here, instead of spending money for a motel." "She?" "A family friend." He looked at his watch. "Wow, look at the time, I...gotta go." Lyn said, "Will we see you again?" "I hope so. I'll call you." He kissed her cheek. "Bye for now."

Leon said, "I don't trust him. He's up to something. It's in his eyes. Notice how he never quite looks you straight in the eye. And another thing, as suddenly as he came, he's gone again. I don't trust anyone that disappears as fast or as much as this guy does." Dre said, "I agree with Leon. Something 's fishy about him, even if he is cute." "Well I know one thing for sure. Next time, I'm gonna follow him and check his story out."

Lynetta said, "Oh you guys, you're so suspicious of every guy I know." Dre said, "Not like this one. He really creeps me out " "And me too. Hey, if I'm wrong I'll apologize. But...what if I'm not?" Lynetta said, "Okay, let's take the food back to Jack's apartment and I'll make coffee." Dre said, "Sounds great to me." Leon said, "Alright, but let's stop and get some more O. J. I drank the last of it last night." "Okay then, let's go."

Ronny thought to himself, "Wow that was close. I don't know how long I can keep this up. But I have to. I need the money. I only hope she doesn't find out what's really going on. I'd better go."

Back to Jack: Knock Knock, "Jack, are you almost done?" He stopped concentrating on Lyn, "Yeah sorry, it's just that the hot water felt so good I lost track. I'll be out soon. (Hurry Baby L, I miss you and I need you.) Jack got out, dried off and dressed, all the time hoping he got through to Lynetta.

He walked out and Sylvia was waiting. "Wow you really are...uh hungry?" (that's not what she was going to say.) "Yes, I am." "Well I think I'll let you eat in the dinning room this morning." "Thanks." They went out to the dinning room and there was a ton of food on the table. "I wasn't sure what you'd like so I made a variety for you." In a surprised tone, "*You made* all of this for me?" "Did I forget to say I like to cook." "I think you forgot that little bit of information." "Well have a seat and help yourself or would you like me to serve you?" "Uh, no. I think I can manage, thanks." She sat across from him sipping her coffee and watching him which made Jack very nervous. After 2 bites he pushed his plate back and said, "I'm sorry I'm not as hungry as I thought. I'll just drink some O.J." "But I made all of this for you." "I know and I'm sorry. I just can't...eat." "You ate fine last night in your room." "But I didn't see people watching me. It's different."

"Okay, (talking to the guards), you 3 go take a break for 1 hour. You can all go somewhere but be back in 1 hour." One of them said, "But shouldn't one of us-" "No, it'll be fine. Just go but remember 1 hour." So the 3 guards left. "There, is that better?" "It's a start." "What else can I do?" "You could make him leave." "No he has to stay, sorry." "Then can he at least turn the other way?" To the guard: "You heard him, turn around. Now anything else?" He thought for a few seconds then he looked at Sylvia and said, "Do you *have* to sit at the end of the table looking at me over your coffee cup? My mom used to do that." "Would you rather I went into the other room?"

Again he thought for a few seconds, "How can I gain her trust more?" Then Jack spoke to her in a low, soft voice, "No Sylvia. (Jack walked over to her, brushed her hair behind one shoulder and took her hand) I would much rather have you come over here and sit by me. I don't bite, much. (Then he winked at her.) He pulled a chair out, next to him, for her to sit in and kissed the back of her hand. "Would you like something from the table, Sylvia?" His face was inches from hers as he ran his fingers through her hair. She looked into his piercing blue eyes, closed her eyes and took a deep breath. Jack leaned over like he was going to kiss her and she felt his breath on her face, but then instead, he served her a few things from the huge spread on the table and then he fed her a small bite of a biscuit. He sat down and said, "I think I can eat now." Then he winked at her again as he slowly took a small bite of the same biscuit.

*What is happening? Is Jack being taken in by Sylvia? Does she have some kind of spell cast on him?*

*Has he forgotten all about Lynetta? Read on and find out the answers in the next episode.*

# Seven

## (Part 2)
## Jack is Still Missing

After breakfast was over Jack stretched and said, "*That*- was delicious. What other surprises do you have hidden away?" "Oh just wait and see. You'll find I'm full of surprises." "I can't wait. I think I'll take a little nap. Thanks for a wonderful breakfast." He kissed the back of her hand again, ran his finger lightly down her cheek and went back into his room. Sylvia had decided to keep the guard outside the room rather than inside so Jack could have some privacy and to keep the two of them from talking and getting too chummy. Jack laid on his bed and closed his eyes. Soon a smile came to his lips and he said her name over and over again, "Sylvia, Sylvia, Sylvia." and thought very hard.

Just then Ronny pulled up to his friend's house, gave the special knock then waited to be let in. The guard looked out, saw Ronny and let him in. Ronny went to Sylvia, "Sylvia, I'm not sure I can do this." "What do you mean? Wait a minute. (She checked on Jack and closed his door, but she was unaware that it didn't latch, so it opened just a crack. Jack heard voices so he got up and listened at the door.)

Okay, what do you mean, you're not sure you can do this? You told me you've wanted this girl for so long and now she's right within your grasp. Her boyfriend is safely out of the way, so what are you waiting for?"

Jack wondered, "Who are they talking about." The guy continued, "I know. But Netta is no ordinary girl, She's... special I can't move too fast. But what bothers me most is her 2 best friends who seem to always be with her, Dre and especially that guy...Leon or something like that. He looks at me like he knows or something." "Well you'd better get a grip on yourself, I'm not waiting on you forever." "I know. So, how 'd this morning go? And where are all the guys?" "Oh I gave them all a one hour break so Jack and I could have a private breakfast, just the two of us."(She smiled) "The two of you, with Tiny here?" (he pointed to the guard) "Oh, I had him turn around." "Well just be careful that Jack isn't playing you for a fool." "No. He's putty in my hands. He...fed me a bit of breakfast and even asked me to sit near him instead of the end of the table." "Maybe but don't forget, he IS an actor." "Go on, go get your Netta or whatever you call her." "Thanks. I will. Later Syl."

Jack was thinking to himself, "So that's what's going on. They're working together to keep Lyn and I apart and for themselves. Okay this mental telepathy stuff *has* to work and NOW! Hurry Baby L, I can't keep up this act for long. You have to find me. I Love You!"

Sylvia noticed Jack's door was slightly open and wondered if he heard Ronny and her talking. She said, "Oh no! I hope he didn't..." As she walked toward the door a floorboard creaked and the 3 other guards came back with the code knock on the front door. Sylvia said to Ronny, "Get that." As Jack quickly laid on the bed and pretended to be asleep, she opened the door quickly, hoping he'd been asleep the whole time. She looked in to see him lying on the bed, apparently sleeping, and went over to him. She reached out to run her fingers through his hair. She hesitated a moment and softly said, "I hope Ronny is wrong about you, I so want you to be mine!"

She ran her fingers through his hair and he pretended to like it. He turned over and dreamily said, "Sylvia, mm, time to get up?" He was stretching, (as if he'd been asleep.) "If you want to." He opened his eyes and looked at her. "Oh, hi. Sylvia, (he gave her a wink and a half a smile) Did you want me...for something?"

Pretending like he was just waking up, he ran his fingers slowly through his hair, knowing it would drive her crazy. She took a deep breath and said, "No, just checking on you." "And?" Then he quickly grabbed her around her waist, pulled her down and tickled her. She screamed with delight and surprise and then laughed as Jack tickled her more, then he said, "Had enough?" She said, "No!" Just then the guard burst through the door, grabbed Sylvia and when she caught her breath, she yelled, "GET OUT!"-to the guard. The guard said, "but..." "I said get out!"

"Sorry!" The guard left and looked at the others with a puzzled look and shrugging his shoulders.

Jack said, "I'm sorry. I just couldn't resist and your perfume smells so good this morning. Again, I'm sorry if I embarrassed you." "You don't have to be sorry, they do. Well the moments gone and I have things to do so, I'll see you later. Bye Jack."

As she was leaving, the guard was ready to be chewed out some more but she just walked past and said, "I'll be back after awhile." Jack began to concentrate on Lyn again.

Back with Leon and Adrianne, they went back to the apartment and Lyn went to the kitchen to make coffee. Suddenly, while she was measuring the coffee, Jack's face appeared in front of her. He looked desperate. Then she saw him reaching out, as if toward her. She dropped the coffee and reached back to him as if he was standing right there. He seemed to be saying help me, then he was gone. She screamed, "Jack, don't go."

Leon and Adrianne rushed into the kitchen and found Lyn crying and coffee was all over the sink. She appeared to be reaching toward the window. Together they asked, "What happened?" Lynetta crumbled to the floor in tears, "Jack's in real trouble. He's trying to reach me. We can't wait. We have to call the police now." Adrianne said, "Okay We'll call. What was the officer's name?"

"Detective Sargent Lynn Shelby, tell her it's urgent."

"Detective Lynn Shelby, got it." While Adrianne made the call, Leon helped Lynetta to the couch. Lynetta apologized for not getting the coffee made and for the mess she made. Leon told her, "Don't worry about that, try to remember everything you saw when you saw Jack. It may help us get him back." "I only saw him looking helpless and lost. And he looked so desperate." "Okay, what else do you remember? Think, think hard." "I... didn't recognize the shirt he had on. It was blue and white striped, I think...oh it's useless. Maybe I'm just imagining it or maybe I'm just going crazy." She started to cry again.

Suddenly Leon said, "No, wait. I think Jack might be trying to use mental telepathy." "What?" "Yeah, we talked about it once after a show we watched. A woman's husband had been kidnapped and every time his captors left him alone he kept sending mental images and thoughts to his wife hoping she would find him. She talked to the police and together they found him and arrested the kidnappers. We laughed and joked about it until we saw the end of the show where they interviewed the actual couple. She said she had never had an experience like that before and not one since he was rescued.

Jack and I looked at each other and freaked out. I was thinking, maybe the love those two had for each other was so strong that it was the key to finding him. I think you and Jack have that same kind of love for each other. I think it's worth a try, don't you?" "I'm not sure. And I wouldn't know how." "Look just sit down and think only of Jack and how much you love him. I know you can do that much." "Alright I'll try."

Adrianne came in with some news, "They're sending over an officer to fill out a missing person report. They should be here soon." Lynetta said, "Thanks Dre." Adrianne said to Leon, "You stay with her, I'm going to clean up the coffee and make a pot." "Alright."

Leon sat next to Lynetta on the couch, pulled her close and put his arm around her. All she could think about was Jack. She called out softly, "Jack, talk to me. Tell me where you are." Leon said, "Shh now. Maybe he doesn't have a clue where he is, But it's obvious, to me, that he wants to come back to you, so you have to know that he still loves you. So stay positive. Try to let *him* know how much *you* love *him* and need him and he'll feel it in his heart wherever he is, I promise." "Thanks Leon I needed to hear that. And I have the greatest friends in the world right here with me." Lynetta started to concentrate on her love for Jack.

Back over with Jack, he was lying on the bed trying to fall asleep when all of a sudden he saw Lynetta's face with a tear falling down her cheek. He saw her looking at something. As it came into view he saw it was a picture of him. He watched her trace the outline of his face with her finger but then he also felt it on his face. He heard her thoughts, "I love you Jack, please come back to me. I'm so lost without you." Then he saw her hugging his picture and crying even harder. "I have to find a way out of here. I have to get back to my baby. She needs me."

At Jack's apartment, Knock, knock, knock. Adrianne went to the door, "I've got it." She opened the door. A police officer was standing there with her badge open. "Hello, I'm Detective Sargent Lynn Shelby, is this the home of a Mr. Jack Zachry?" "Hello, yes it is. I'm Adrianne. Lynetta and Leon are both in the other room. Please come in." "Anything new since I called last?" "I think Jack is trying to reach Lynetta by using mental telepathy." "Oh, why do you say that?" "She told us she could see him but she didn't recognize the shirt he had on, but you should really talk to her."

Detective Sargent Shelby showed her badge to Lynetta and Leon. "I understand you may have had some contact with Jack, is this true?" "Yes. I think he's trying to reach me or I'm just going crazy." "Well, we'll see. Why don't you tell me what you remember and we'll see if we can fill in the missing pieces, okay?"

"Okay. I didn't think you would be the one to come. I mean, I thought you'd send over, you know a regular officer." "Well, I was going to do that but something inside me said, I should handle this case myself." "Thank you." "You can thank me when we get Jack back home where he belongs. Now let's get started."

Detective Shelby was getting the backgrounds on Jack and Lynetta and as much info as she could up to this moment. "Well I think that's enough to get started." They all stood up. Detective Shelby put her arm around Lynetta and gave her a squeeze. "Keep your chin up and stay positive. That's how we'll get him back. And let me know if he tries to contact you again. Remember, love is a powerful force and not many people know how to use its power. We'll talk soon. It was nice to meet all of you. Bye for now." Dre said, "Bye and thanks."

While Detective Shelby was in the apartment Ronny was trying to get the nerve up to call Lynetta. Finally he called. She answered, "Hello?" "Hi Netta, it's Ronny." "Oh hi Ronny." Leon and Dre heard his name and came over.

Ronny said, "How are you?" "Alright I guess?" "Hey can we get together today? I'd love to see you." "I don't know. I'm not good company right now. (Leon and Adrianne both started waving their hands frantically to get Lyn's attention. She looked over at them), "Just a minute Ronny. (She covered the mouthpiece with her hand), what's with you two?" Leon said, "Go ahead and have him come over."

"What, why?" "Just do it. I'll explain later, but just let him think you're only apartment sitting while Jack's *away*." "Okay, Hey Ronny, sorry about the interruption." "Are you sure you don't want me to come over? I might be able to make you feel better." "Well since you put it that way, I guess you can come over for a little while." "Alright I'll see you at your place in half an hour?" "Oh, no, my friends and I are apartment sitting at Jack's while he's away. I'll have to give you directions."

Lynetta gave Ronny directions and said, "Bye, see you soon." "Bye." Ronny jumped into his car and started over to see Lynetta.

Meanwhile, Detective Sargent Shelby went back to the apartment. Knock, knock knock. Adrianne answered the door, "Forget something?" "Yes, could I borrow one of Jack's shirts? Preferably the last one he wore so it still has his scent on it." "Oh sure, here you can take this one, (she grabbed the one off the back of the door.) Anything else?" "No, this is good thanks." She held it away, "Strong scent."

Ronny pulled up and panicked when he saw the police car and an officer coming out of an apartment with some kind of cloth. He waited till the car drove away and then went to look for the apartment. When he got there he realized that it was the same apartment the officer came out of. He knocked and the door opened. Dre said, "Hi Ronny." Hesitantly he said, "Hi is -- Lynetta here?" "Oh yeah, she's sitting on the couch with Leon." "Did I see the police here?" "Yeah, well, you may as well know, our friend Jack is missing and Lynetta is devastated. She's trying to keep it together but she's losing. I think she's about to go over the edge. It's only a matter of time." "But the police?"

Ronny, I don't think you quite understand. Jack and Lynetta are so in love with each other that it seems as if one can't live without the other. They're like two halves and together they make a perfect circle. Lynetta is so lost without him. We had to do something, so we called the police to report him as a missing person."

Ronny went over to Lynetta. The look on her face broke Ronny's heart. He knew she could never feel that kind of love for him. He couldn't keep the charade up any more. But what about Sylvia? She'll kill him if she finds out he told. She said she'd do *anything* to have Jack all to herself. And what will Lynetta think of *him*, she'll hate him There's got to be a way out. He just has to find it.

"Hi Netta." "Oh Hi Ronny." She wiped the tears from her face. "Are you okay? Adrianne filled me in on what's been going on. Can I help?" "Oh Ronny." Lynetta burst into tears. Ronny reached for her and held her tightly as she cried. He thought to himself, "It feels so good to hold you, but, it isn't right. You belong with *him* not me. I have to make it right. Even if it means, that I can't have you and you may hate me forever." Not realizing that he said it out loud, Lynetta heard, "I love you Netta." She said, "What?" "Oh nothing." "But I heard..." "Uh, maybe Jack is trying to reach you again? I have to go now." "No please, stay awhile with me?" "I can't. I really have to go. Goodbye Netta." He whispered, "Don't forget me." Then he kissed her cheek and quickly left, saying goodbye to Leon and Adrianne on his way out.

Leon told Dre, "I'm gonna follow him. He's definitely up to something. Call Detective Shelby and tell her what's going down. I'll be in touch." "Leon, be careful." "I will." They kissed each other goodbye.

Leon got into Jack's car and followed Ronny. Ronny was so upset over Lynetta he was unaware that he was being followed. "Oh no! A yellow light, stay yellow for Lynetta... whew. Thank you. I hope I don't lose this guy."

Clear across town and a little way out in the country they both reached Sylvia's house. Leon stayed at a slight distance, but he could still see where Ronny was going. When Ronny pulled into the driveway of a big house, Leon stopped the car back a ways from view. Ronny got out and looked around. "Yikes." Leon ducked out of sight. Ronny closed his door and headed for the front door of the house. "Whew, that was close." Leon watched Ronny go up to the house and give a special knock. The door opened and he went inside.

Leon thought to himself, "I need some backup." He called Detective Shelby, "Come on pick up..." "Hello, Detective Sargent Shelby's office, may I help you?" "I need to speak to Detective Shelby, it's urgent. My name is Leon. Please hurry." "I think she's gone for the day but I'll check. Please hold." "Please be there." "This is Detective Sargent Shelby, is this Leon?" "Yes." "Okay, fill me in, what's going on?" "I think I know where Jack is." "Wait, slow down. How? Are you sure?" Leon told Detective Sargent Shelby about his suspicions concerning Ronny and where he had followed him to.

"Alright I believe you, BUT, we have to do this by the book, if we want it to stick. So stay put and wait until I get there. I'm bringing the K-9 unit. I have Jack's shirt. If he's in there we'll find him but right now I need you to be my eyes and ears, so don't do *anything* before we get there." "Okay but hurry. There's not much of a hiding place out here." "I will and Leon?" "What?" "I don't need any dead heroes on my hands. SO SIT TIGHT! Goodbye."

Detective Sargent Shelby got her officers together and quickly gave them the low down. "Let's move."

Ronny went in to talk to Sylvia. Jack heard muffled voices and went to the door. "What are we going to do?" "Are you sure they were coming from HIS apartment?" "Yes. The girl, Adrianne told me." "Did any of them follow you?" "No. I'm sure. They were too busy looking after Netta. They don't have time to chase after me." "Okay. It looks like we have to change houses and fast. Get everything ready. It will be dark soon so hurry I don't want a surprise visit from the cops. Get the chloroform, we don't need any resistance from Jack." Ronny went after the chloroform. Sylvia looked at everyone, "Alright, everyone knows what to do right?" They all agreed. The police were just arriving around the corner, out of sight of the house.

Leon saw the SWAT team exit the van without a sound and the K-9 unit pulled in behind. Just a few feet away from him Detective Sargent Shelby got out of her unmarked police car. Leon called to her as quietly as he could, "Lynn, it's Leon, behind you." She turned around and made her way back to him. Any new developments Leon?" "No. The house is quiet, almost too quiet if you know what I mean." "I know what you mean. We'll wait for everyone to get into position and then we move.

Inside the house, Jack said to himself, "They're not going to take me without a fight." Sylvia said to Ronny, "It's time. Go get Jack." Ronny took the chloroform to Jack's room. He quietly opened the door, but Jack was behind it. Ronny's heart was pounding. Jack wasn't on the bed so Ronny looked over at the bathroom. He started towards it. Jack tapped him on the shoulder as Ronny turned Jack tried to punch him but Ronny dodged out of the way. The door slammed shut as Ronny pinned Jack to the door and locked it.

Ronny covered Jack's mouth and said as quietly as he could, "Wait a minute Jack, just listen to me for one minute and then if you want to you can punch my lights out. But if you want to get out of here and back to Lynetta we have to work together. Sylvia has lost her mind. She wants you at any cost. She'd even kill Lynetta if it meant she could have you all to herself. Now I love Netta but she loves you so much and after what I saw today, well, your disappearance has really hit her hard. So I decided to help *her* get *you* back but if Sylvia knows I'm helping you she'll kill me. Now, do we work together or what?"

Jack narrowed his eyes at Ronny and said, "I still don't trust you, but I guess I don't have a choice. Do you have a plan?" "Here it is, I'm supposed to use chloroform to knock you out, cover you with a blanket, then carry you out to her car and put you into the back seat. *My* plan is: you *pretend* to be knocked out, I carry out the rest of the plan to get you to the car. Once you're in the back seat give me a few moments to see if the guys are watching and when the coast is clear you sneak out and head for home and back to Netta. Now, here's a map telling you where you are, (he pulled a map out of his shirt,) Okay, got it?"

"Got it, but what about you? What's to keep you from coming after Lynetta again later?" "You Jack. I know now that she's in love with you and I'm just a part of her past and that's where I'll stay as long as *you* make her happy. So lets do this for Ness I mean for Lynetta." "Thanks man, let's go."

Jack laid on the bed like he was out cold. The guys were pounding on the door and yelling, "Ronny what's going on?" Ronny unlocked the door and pretended that he had to fight Jack to use the chloroform and he pretended to be a little out of breath. "It's okay now. He was pretty strong, but he's out like a light now."

Sylvia said to one of the other guys, "You, take him and put him in my car." Ronny said, "Wait, I'm supposed to do that." "No, I have another job for you." "Why change the plan now?" "I just thought after your little scuffle with Jack you'd rather let someone else take him out. After all he'll be dead weight, now that he's out." "But my adrenaline is like way up now. I think I could lift even Tiny there." "Okay, take Jack out as planned."

Outside the police were all in place and the signal was given. Just then Ronny came out with Jack over his shoulder covered in a blanket. He made his way to Sylvia's car opened the back door and started to put Jack inside. Just as he put Jack down and looked around Ronny said, "All clear Jack."

Then Suddenly someone from behind said, "Hands behind your head." Ronny turned around to see a police officer with a hand gun pointed right at him, "Wait, wait a minute. It's not what you think. Jack get up." Jack got up and threw off the blanket. The officer was taken by surprise. "What? What's going on?"

Jack told the officer, "Hey, he's okay! He helped me escape. It's the people inside you need to get. And the leader is a woman named Sylvia, She's crazy, man." "What's your name?" "Jack Zachry." "Are you hurt at all?" "No. I'm okay." The officer got on his radio, "Detective Shelby I have the victim secured." "Roger that. Alright everyone lets do this. Move in, now." All the officers were swarming over the place. Just as the guys were coming out the police stepped out and announced, "Police, you're under arrest, come on out with your hands up."

One by one as the guys came out they were handcuffed.

Detective Sargent Shelby came over and asked the first guy, "Okay where's your ring leader?" There was no answer from any of them. "Okay get the dogs. I really wish you wouldn't make me do this... alright, on my signal, release the dogs." "Wait, wait." "Hold the dogs! Start talking and remember this is your bosses last chance."

"What will happen to her?" "We'll decide that later but first we have to get her into custody." Just then, over the radio, "Detective Sargent Shelby, we have a female suspect in custody, over." "Roger that. Send in the dogs to check for anyone else." They sent in the dogs and found no one else in the house. So they sealed off the house as a crime scene. Detective Sargent Shelby announced to everyone over the radio, "Great job everyone. Let's wrap it up and go home. See you back at the station."

Detective Sargent Shelby walked over to Jack and Ronny. "Well you boys have had quite an adventure." She turned toward Jack. "You must be Jack." "Yes ma'am." She put out her hand to shake his. I'm Detective Sargent Lynn Shelby, it's nice to meet you. I know a certain young lady who's going to be extremely glad to see you again!" Jack smiled. "But don't you need a statement or something?" "All I need for tonight is to know, were you held against your will?" "Yes I was." "Okay that's enough to hold all of them for 24 hours for kidnapping. We can take your statement tomorrow. I can send an officer to your home or you can come down to the station but you can decide tomorrow which you want to do. You can just give the station a call and let us know what you decided."

Just then an officer brought Sylvia, now handcuffed, over to a police unit. Jack looked at her and shook his head. Sylvia tried to blow him a kiss just before they put her in the car. The unit pulled away and Jack watched till it was out of sight.

Leon asked the Detective, "Can I take Jack home now?" "Of course. We'll even give you a police escort to get you there faster. Leon, it was a pleasure. Have you ever considered a job with the police force? You'd be good at surveillance. You really know how to keep a cool head in the heat of the moment." "No. I've always wanted to dance not be a policeman." "Well, I want to give you something as a special reward for tonights work." She reached into her car and handed something to Leon and to Jack. They looked at their gifts. They each held a badge that read: Honorary Police Officer badge #001. Jack said, "Thanks." Leon said, "Uh, yeah, thanks." Detective Shelby said, "Now get out of here both of you." Jack had an after thought, "Detective?" "Yes?" "What will happen to Ronny? I mean He did help me escape." "We'll question him and hold him for 24 hours, a lot depends on your statement and how well he cooperates with us. We'll see tomorrow how it goes. Go on home now. Let her know you're okay." "Okay. Thanks."

Leon gave Jack a big hug and said, "It's your car, want to drive?" "No dude I just want to see..." "Say no more. We'll be there soon." The police car pulled away and Leon followed. As soon as the car started to roll Jack turned toward the window to hide his tears. He thought to himself, "Baby L, I'm coming home to you." He put his head down and sobbed thinking how close he came to not seeing Lyn ever again. When he got control again Leon asked, "You okay dude?" "Yeah, thanks." "We're almost there. Soon she'll be back in your arms." "I know. I just can't believe it. Not yet."

As they got closer the officer turned off the siren and the lights so Jack could surprise her. Leon parked the car and just sat there. Jack said, "Come on dude we're here." "No man, You don't need me there. It's enough that Adrianne is there." "Dude would you come on. I want you there and Lynetta will want to thank you too." "Okay but I'm not staying long." "Whatever. Just get out here." They waved to the officer as they went up the stairs.

Leon went in first. He opened the door, the girls looked up and saw Leon walk in. He stepped aside and Jack walked in. Adrianne screamed and Lynetta jumped to her feet and fainted. Jack picked her up and put her on the couch. Adrianne went and got a cool, wet cloth and handed it to Jack. He put it on her forehead and kissed her. Then he called to her, "Baby L, wake up honey, it's me, I'm really here. Wake up, come on. Open those beautiful brown eyes for me." She began to wake up so he kept talking to her. She reached up to touch his face, "Are you really here?" "Yes baby! I'm really here. I'm not going anywhere, not without you. I love you sooo much. I tried to reach you by just concentrating on you but..." "Me too." "Really?" "Where'd this shirt come from?" "They gave it to me, why?" "I saw you earlier today wearing that shirt but I had never seen it before now. I don't understand."

"Well, speaking about things you don't understand, I thought I heard you say, 'I love you Jack, please come back to me, I'm so lost without you' and I saw you holding my picture and tracing the outline of my face but the weird thing is, I actually felt your finger on my face, then I figured it must be my imagination because I missed you so much." "But I *did* say that and I *did* trace your face with my finger, was it this picture?" She showed him the picture she had been holding. "Yes! That's the one I saw." "But how?" "I guess we love each other so much that we can hear or see each other wherever we are." Leon and Adrianne sneaked out and went home so Jack and Lynetta could be alone.

Lynetta got up and Jack said, "Where are you going?" "It's late and you're home safe and sound so I thought I should go home now so you can get some sleep." "Don't go! Stay tonight. I just want to feel you in my arms tonight. I want to wake up and know this isn't just a dream. Please, stay with me?" "Are you sure?" "I'm sure. Hey where are Leon and Adrianne?" "They left awhile ago so we could be alone together." "I'll have to remember to thank them." "Me too." "Come here you." Jack pulled Lyn back on the couch with him, wrapped her up in his arms and cuddled and nuzzled her. Happy to be back together they fell asleep.

The next morning Jack woke up and smiled at Lynetta still cradled in his arms. He leaned over and softly kissed her. She stirred and slowly opened her eyes. She smiled up at Jack, then they kissed. He said, "Good morning, beautiful."

"Good morning handsome." "I'm so glad you're here, in my arms. This is right where you belong. You know, I have some unfinished business to do today?" "What?" "I have to give the police my statement, either here or the station. But I don't want to leave you." "Neither do I." "Then it's settled I'll do it here." Jack called the police station, "Hi, my name is Jack Zachry and I need to give a statement about last nights arrest of Sylvia." "Who was the officer in charge?" "Detective Sargent Shelby." "One moment please, I believe she wanted to speak to you if you called." "Okay."

"Jack, I want to commend you once again on how smoothly things went last night and no one was injured. However I do have some disturbing news to tell you. Could you come down to the station this morning?

"I have my girlfriend Lynetta here and I really don't want to leave her today." "Well you should bring her along. This also concerns her. I understand she was acquainted with the young man who helped you escape last night?" "I'm not sure, I'd have to ask her."

"Would you please bring her with you and let's finish this conversation here. I think it would be best that way. You'll understand when you get here. See you soon?" "Alright we'll be down in say 1 hour? We just got up." " One hour? That will be fine. See you both then."

Jack and Lynetta had breakfast then off to the police station. Lynetta said, "I wonder why she wants me there?

"Lyn, there's something I didn't tell you, about my disappearance, because I never thought you'd need to know." "What?" "Do you know a guy named Ronny?" She looked at him with a strange look and answered hesitantly. "Yes, when I was a kid, why?"

"You never asked me how I got away last night." "I was just so glad to have you back I didn't think about it. How did you get away?" "Ronny. He was part of the whole scheme." "No. Not Ronny?" "I'm afraid so, starting with supposedly running into you at the park and kissing you."

Jack told her all he knew as he drove to the police station. Lynetta found it so hard to believe. "There's the police station. You ready?" "I guess so. It's just so hard to believe, about Ronny I mean. But I guess It explains why he showed up so suddenly after all these years. I also want to put in a good word for him toward his defense, after all he did help you to escape and come back to me." "That's true. We'll see what we can do to help Ronny. He really does care about you. Well, let's go see what Detective Shelby wants."

They went in and found Detective Shelby's office. She greeted them at the door, "Hi, thank you both for coming so quickly. Can I get you two something to drink?" Jack looked at Lynetta and both said, "No thanks." "Well, let's get to it. I asked *you* here Lynetta because I have some disturbing news for you and there's just no easy way to say it, so I'm just going to say it straight out. The young man who helped Jack escape last night, was found in his cell this morning." Lynetta gasped and said, "Ronny?" "Yes. I'm sorry I have to tell you this, he committed suicide last night. He left notes for each of you. Understand, we have to keep them as evidence for now, but you can read them." Lyn asked, "Could someone have...you know..." "I don't think so. I think he had it planned in advance. Considering what is written in each of the notes, they were written quite recently but were well thought out and the handwriting was not done in a hurry, that much is obvious."

Lynetta and Jack were each handed a plastic bag containing a sheet of paper. They began to read their notes.

*Dear Netta,*
*If you're reading this then I'm dead. But I couldn't leave you without telling you how much I've always loved you. It broke my heart when we moved away all those years ago. I'd always hoped we would some how get back together. But I see now it wasn't meant to be. Jack is truly a wonderful guy who loves you with all his heart and I know you feel the same way about him. So I know you will be well cared for and loved. I only wish it could have been you and me. But if you're truly happy with Jack that's good enough for me and I can die a happy man. You're the only woman I ever wanted. I don't want to go on without you in my life. I'm so sorry I hurt you. I hope you can find it in your heart to forgive me, even though I know I don't deserve it. Please remember me as I was when we were kids and not the way I turned out. And remember I will always love you. Goodbye.*
*All My Love,*
*Ronny*

Lynetta cried while reading her letter. Then Jack read Ronny's letter to him.

*Jack,*
*I'm truly sorry for what I put you and Lynetta through. We both love*

*Lynetta very much but she's very much in love with you. I see that now. I'm only sorry I didn't see it sooner. Love makes you do some strange things. I know I don't have to say it, except for my sake, please take care of Lynetta. I'm counting on you. I hope you two will always be happy together. Don't worry, I won't be around to mess it up. I wish you and Netta all the best. Goodbye.*
*Ronny*

Jack looked over and saw Lynetta still crying and put his arms around her to comfort her. He grabbed a tissue from the desk and wiped her tears. She clutched the note to her in disbelief. Jack said to her, "Deep down inside he was a good man who loved you. But he saw how much you love me and gave up his pursuit of you. His pain must have been more than he could take to cause him to take his own life. Well he's at peace now, and he asked me to take care of you, so we have his blessing. Here, you can read what he wrote to me. Maybe it will make you feel...a little better."

Jack handed her his note. "And here, you can read mine." She handed Jack her note. After reading what Ronny had written to Jack she could almost manage half a smile. When they were finished reading They handed the notes back to Detective Shelby. "You may have these back after we're finished with them. She put her hand on Lynetta's. "He really did love you but sometimes it isn't meant to be. He took the wrong path and made some wrong choices, but he tried to make up for it by giving Jack back to you. You should take some comfort in that. Now let's get your statement young man, so you kids can go home."

Jack gave his statement. They said their thanks and goodbyes and headed for home. Jack and Lynetta looked up to the sky and both of them whispered, "Thanks Ronny."

# Eight

## Lost in a Kiss

Jack, Leon and Brian headed to the Corner Coffee Shoppe just to hang out together. Lynetta, Alyssa and Adrianne were shopping at the mall.

Three girls walked into the Coffee Shoppe for coffee. One of them recognized Leon from a video he had made and she wanted to say Hi but she was too shy. She nudged her friend Salena and nodded toward Leon and whispered, "That's him!" So Salena went up to Leon for her and boldly said, "Hey, are you Leon James?" He smiled at her and said, "Yes I am, what's your name?" "Well I'm Salena, but you see, my friend Shondra over there, saw you in a video and she recognized you when we came in. She's a <u>big</u> fan of yours and she'd like to say Hi but she's too shy so could you, you know come over and say Hi to her?" "Sure. I like to meet my fans. I'll be right over."

Leon excused himself from the guys and he took his drink over with him. "Hi, Shondra is it? I'm Leon. I heard you're a fan of mine and you like one of my videos." "Well actually I like all the videos you've made and I'm trying to collect all the songs you've done. I really enjoy listening to you sing. I especially like the last one you made." "Really? Me too. I had a lot of fun doing that one. I wish I had a copy with me, I'd autograph it for you." "You would?" "Sure."

Leon and Shondra went over and sat on one of the corner couches to talk some more while her friends sat with Jack and Brian. Everyone was having a wonderful time.

After awhile Jack said, "Ladies this has been great but we have to go now. I'm sorry." "Aw, do you have to?" "Yeah we do. Hey, Leon, time to go." "Okay dude." Jack said, "Maybe we'll see you ladies again?"

"Shondra, I had a great time. Can I call you sometime?" "But don't you have a girlfriend? I mean, what about Adrianne?" "Oh Adrianne and I are friends, but we're not, you know, dating. Adrianne's someone I can hang out with cause she's pretty much in the same boat. I've been too busy to have a steady girlfriend. But things are kind of quiet right now, so maybe that can change. Do you know anyone who would like to go out with me?" "Maybe?" "Just maybe?" "Well I know I would." "Really? Can I have your number then?" "Sure. It's 555-2432." He wrote it on his napkin and drew a heart around it. "See you later Shondra." Then he kissed the back of her hand and she left with her friends.

Brian came over and asked, "What was all the hand kissing for?" "I just want her to remember me till next time."

Jack said, "Next time? What is it with you and the 'ladies man' thing? You're like a magnet." "Yeah well, you know...when you got it, hey she's fun and easy to talk to." Brian and Jack together said, "And pretty." "Really? I hadn't noticed. (he smiled) Alright let's go."

Just as they walked out Jarrod was coming down the sidewalk. "Hey guys what's shakin'?" "Hey dude." Brian said, "We just had something to drink. We haven't decided what to do but now that you're here, how about a game of 2 on 2, guys?" They all said, "Yeah, sounds great." Jarrod said, "I'll grab something and meet you on the court." Jack said, "Alright, but hurry." Soon all 4 guys were on the B-ball court and the game began.

The girls finished their shopping and headed to the Corner Coffee Shoppe, everyones favorite hangout. They each ordered their coffee or whatever and sat down for a much needed rest. Adrianne was looking at the magazines on the coffee table when a paper napkin with writing on it caught her eye. She picked it up for a closer look. There was a heart drawn on it and inside the heart was: Leon and Shondra Forever-Love and XO. Adrianne smiled, "Oh look another fan showing her undying love for Leon." She showed it to Lynetta who said, "How cute.

I guess if we're going to date America's teen heartthrobs we'd better get used to stuff like that." "I guess so." Lynetta saw something on the other side. "Hey Dre what's on the other side?" "Huh?" She turned the napkin over. "I don't know, looks like a phone number. It says 555-243 something. The last number must have gotten wet. I can't make it out. Oh well, it's not like she actually gave it to him. I mean it was just laying here on the table, right?"

She never gave it a second thought. They all finished their drinks or almost. Adrianne took hers up to the counter to get a refill and a lid. She laid the napkin on the counter and waited for her coffee. They were brewing a fresh pot for her while she waited. While she was waiting Leon walked in and saw the girls. He looked surprised to see them.

"Uh, Hi girls. How was the shopping?" From the couch, where the girls were sitting rubbing their feet, they said, "Exhausting but lots of fun. How about you guys? What'd you do today? Hey where *are* the others?" "We were here for awhile then we went to play 2 on 2 when Jarrod came by."

Leon went over to where he was sitting earlier and tried to look casually at the magazines without appearing to be looking for something. He looked on the floor. Then he pretended to drop something and felt around on the floor, nothing.

Adrianne said, "Did you happen to meet anyone new today?" "Huh, me? Uh, I meet new people all the time." "Did you meet any girls today?" "Oh yeah, now that I think about it, there were some girls that came in after we got our drinks. We were polite and said hi."

The guy behind the counter started to clean off the counter and saw the number on the napkin. He turned it over and read the other side. He saw Leon's name on it and said, "Hey Leon did you drop this?"

Everyone looked over to the counter and Leon tried to signal the guy to hide the napkin or something so the girls, especially Adrianne, wouldn't see it. Too late. The guy saw the look on Adrianne's face and then the look on Leon's face and said, "Remember? You said you'd call my little sister and say hi. She thinks she's in love with you but what does a seven year old know about being in love?"

As the girls all turned to look at Leon the guy winked at him before turning away. Leon walked over to get the napkin. The girls were all teasing Leon, "Aw, how sweet, it's puppy love." Then Adrianne had an idea, turned around and said to the guy, "So, what's your sister's name?" Suddenly Leon's heart sank and he cringed as he picked up the napkin. He thought, "I'm toast." But just then the guy turned around and said, "Shondra, why?" "Oh, just curious. That's so nice of you Leon. I know how fond you are of kids."

Leon said, "You know it. Kids are great. And you know how I love to meet my youngest fans. Well ladies, if you're ready to go I'll escort you to your cars." "Always the gentleman aren't you?" said Adrianne. "You know it."

Leon started to walk out with them and said, "I'll be right there." He went back to the counter and quickly said, "Thanks man I owe you. (then to the girls,) Okay, here we go." And off they went. Leon walked them to their cars. Just before Dre got into hers she looked at Leon and said, "Thank you Leon, you're so sweet." She gave him a big kiss, then she casually said, "Oh, by the way I'm free tomorrow if you don't have any plans."

He tried not to look surprised and said, "Okay, I'll try to remember that, goodbye." "Goodbye Leon." Then they both headed for home.

Next morning Leon woke up with a huge smile on his face. He looked over and saw Shondra's heart drawing on the napkin. He picked it up and kissed it then held it close to him. He laid there remembering when they met and then their conversation and how cute she looked drawing on the napkin. Then the way she blushed when he asked to see what she was drawing. He thought: how sweet and innocent. Suddenly his thoughts were interrupted when his phone rang. He jumped up to answer it. "Hello?" "Leon?" "Yeah, hey Dre, what's up?" "Your home. Where'd you go earlier?" "Nowhere. I just got up." "Sleeping in again? Do you feel okay? It's nearly 9:00." "I'm fine. I didn't have anywhere to be for once so I just thought I'd take it easy and hang out here today."

"Would you like some company? I could bring you some coffee and something for breakfast if you want. We haven't done much lately with our schedules being so crazy, what do you say?" "Oh, I don't know Dre. I just kind of wanted a quiet day to relax, you know? I don't get many days like this." "Sure, get some rest and call me if you change your mind, okay?" "Sure and thanks Dre, you're a good friend. Bye now." "Bye Leon," She blew him a kiss before she hung up. Leon looked confused.

His phone rang again. "Hello?" "Hey dude, it's Jack. Who were you talking to?" "Adrianne called, say have you noticed anything different about her lately?" "What do you mean?" "I don't know exactly. I just feel like…" "Like what Leon? Talk to me." "It's like she thinks we're still, you know dating or something." "Well, did you two actually break up or just kind of stop seeing each other because you both were so busy?" "I guess I never really thought about it."

"Well it looks like she has and it sounds to me like she doesn't think you two are over yet." "But Jack I was gonna call Shondra today and make a date with her."

"So, do it." "But I just told Dre I wanted a quiet day to relax so she wouldn't come over. What if she finds out about Shondra?" "Mm that could be quite a problem." "I know, so can you help me out here?" "Well Adrianne is a mature person. Just tell her the truth. You met a fan you would like to go out with and you thought she'd understand." "Jack, she may be mature but she's also a female. I don't need the drama." "Then I don't know what to tell you, except, you know how Dre feels about people telling the truth." "Yeah, I know. I'm just afraid this time the truth will hurt her a lot and I don't want to do that." "But Leon, what if you go out with Shondra and she found out later?" "Oh dude, I don't even want to think about that. But you're right. I should just tell her. Thanks man." "Anytime dude. Let me know how it goes." "You know it. Later Jack." "Bye Leon." They hung up.

Leon called Dre, "Hello?" "Hi Adrianne, it's Leon." "Oh hi Leon, what's up?" " I need to talk to you. Can we meet somewhere?" "Sure, where?" "The Corner Coffee Shoppe in an hour?" "Okay. See you then." Dre hung up and thought about the sound of Leon's voice. It sounded strangely different. Almost like he was worried about something. She got ready to go and left.

She arrived first and Leon was there shortly after her. He walked in, she was all dressed up and looked beautiful. He thought to himself, "Why did she have to do that? Now it's going to be that much harder to say what I have to."

He walked over to her and she stood up. "Hi Adrianne, thanks for coming." "Hi Leon." "What can I get you, coffee, juice, a pastry?" "Coffee's good." "You go find us a place to sit and I'll be right there."

Leon ordered 2 coffees and joined Adrianne on the corner couch. Leon was very fidgety and nervous so Adrianne took his hands in hers and said, "Leon, we've been friends a long time now. I hope we can tell each other anything, no matter what it is or how painful it may be." "I don't know the right words to say and I've tried so many different ways in my head but the ending is always the same and I can't bear that."

"Then it has something to do with me, doesn't it?" Leon nodded his head but he couldn't look at Adrianne. "I knew there was something I just didn't know what. You've been acting so strangely to me but I thought you'd finally tell me. So...tell me. It'll be okay."

He took a deep breath, "Okay, here goes. Yesterday, while you girls were shopping and I was here with the guys, I met this incredible girl and we talked for quite awhile. Well, you and I haven't been, you know, on a date for some time now, so I just assumed we were just friends now. So I..." "Go on, you what?" "I told her I'd call her up for a date. I'm sorry. I didn't know you still had feelings for me. I wouldn't hurt you for the world, you know that, don't you?"

Adrianne saw the tears in his eyes and tried to comfort him while fighting back her own tears. She took a deep breath and swallowed hard. "Leon, look at me." He looked up into her eyes filled with compassion and understanding. "If you want to take this girl out maybe you should. Perhaps we've taken our friendship for granted and maybe this is just the kind of test we need to see where we both stand. So go ahead and take her out with my blessings. Just remember, I'll always be there for you. We'll always have a special bond no one can break, it's called friendship."

"How did you get to be so incredibly wise, as well as beautiful?" She shrugged her shoulders. They gave each other a big bear hug. "Now, go call this girl and make that date." She winked at Leon who then reached over and kissed her cheek. "Thanks Adrianne, you're wonderful." "Yeah that's what everyone says. Now get out of here."

Leon went home and called Shondra. "Hello?" "Hi Shondra, this is Leon." "Oh hi Leon." "Are you busy tonight? I thought we could go to dinner and a movie if you want to." "Wow, that sounds great. What time?" "I could pick you up at six?" "Alright, 6:00. It's a date. Let me give you directions to my house." Leon got the directions and said, "See you at 6:00," then he hung up.

He was so excited he could hardly wait till it was time to get ready for his date. He decided to take a ball and go shoot some hoops for awhile. Afterwards he went back home to shower and get ready for his big date with Shondra.

Leon was almost ready when his phone rang. He answered, "Hello?" "Dude, you never called me back. What happened with Adrianne? How'd she take it?" "Oh Hi Jack. She took it a lot better than I thought she would and you were right. Being honest is the best way to go with Adrianne." "So when are you going out with this foxy lady?" "Tonight. I'm just finishing getting ready. I'm picking her up at 6:00." "Alright Leon. Have a great time. I'm happy for you." "Thanks man. I'll call you tomorrow and fill you in, on most of it anyway. Later Dude." "Yeah, later."

Soon after they hung up Leon left for his date. He picked up Shondra and they went to dinner. Leon got out and opened her door and then offered her his hand. After dinner they went to a movie and they held hands. But halfway through he did manage to slip his arm around her shoulders.

After the movie he asked if she wanted to go for coffee or something and she said, "Yes." They went to their favorite coffee shop and sat on the couch talking and getting to know each other. Leon really liked it when she laid her head against his shoulder. Once when she did he said, "I could sit like this all night with you." But all too soon it was time to take Shondra home.

When they got to her house she looked at him and said, "I had a really wonderful time, thanks." "Me too. I'd like to take you out again." "I'd like that." "How does Friday night sound?" "Friday night is just fine." "6:00 okay?" "Six is good." "Alright, It's a date and next time I'm gonna take you dancing, instead of to a movie, if you'd like." "Oh, I'd love to go dancing with you. You're an awesome dancer." "Thanks, so I'll see you Friday night." He walked her to her door, then he slowly leaned toward her and softly said, "Goodnight my lady." Then he gently kissed the back of her hand. She went inside and Leon went home.

The next morning Leon woke up with his arms wrapped around his pillow, a smile on his face and someone pounding on his door. He got up and threw on a shirt to answer the door. "Hey Jack, come on in. What's up dude?" he said with a yawn. "Did I wake you up? I can come back if it's too early for you." "No, it's okay, I'll just make some coffee. I was out late with Shondra last night." "So, how was it?" "Oh man, she is so amazing. She makes me feel so...awesome." "So, you had a good time last night. And...are you taking her out again?" "Yep.

Friday night. I'm taking her to dinner and dancing. Hey why don't I call her up and see if she'd like to double with you and Lynetta? That is if you don't have any other plans." "No, I don't, sounds great. I'll call Lynetta and invite her." "And I'll call Shondra." "Leon, what time?" "Six." The guys made their calls.

Lynetta and Shondra both happily accepted. Jack said to Lynetta, "Okay it's a date. I'll pick you up Friday night. Bye." Leon was just finishing his phone call to Shondra. "Alright!" The guys looked at each other and gave each other a high five. Jack said, "Hey let's go shoot some hoops." "Great idea. Let's go."

Jack and Leon went out and spent the afternoon shooting hoops. After a few hours in the hot sun and playing hard, Leon said to Jack, "Let's go get something to drink at The Corner Coffee Shoppe." "Alright." They hung out at the coffee shop then they decided it was time to go home. Leon said, "I'll see you later Jack." "Okay dude. See ya later then."

The week seemed to take forever for Leon. He could hardly wait for Friday night so he could take Shondra out again. It was Wednesday and Leon couldn't wait any longer. He called Shondra. "Hello?" "Hi Shondra. It's Leon." "Oh, hi. I was just thinking about you." "Really? Well I've been thinking about you all week. Are you going to make me wait till Friday to see you or can I see you tonight?" "Well, I should make you wait, but...I want to see you too, so what time?" "How about right now? I could come over and we could go for a walk." "Oh I like that. I'll be waiting. Goodbye." "Okay, I'll be right over. See ya'."

Leon went up to Shondra's door and just before he knocked the door opened. "Wow you weren't kidding when you said you'd be waiting." "Well, I missed you too." Leon smiled at her and they went for their walk. As they started walking Leon slipped his arm around her waist. In a couple of hours they came to a bench. Leon asked, "Would you like to sit for awhile?" "I'd love to." Just as they sat down they both heard some music from somewhere. Leon recognized the song and started to sing. Then he turned to face Shondra and sang to her. At the end of the song he leaned toward her and gave her a long and passionate kiss. "Girl I don't know what it is that you do to me but I hope this feeling never, ever goes away."

"I know what you mean. You make me feel like nobody ever has before and I don't want it to stop. When it's time to leave you it makes me kind of sad inside." "Me too. I find myself wishing I could just stay and never leave. But it's getting late and we both need our sleep. So I'd better walk you home."

At her door he gave her a goodbye kiss on her cheek and a hug. "See you Friday babe." "Thanks for coming over. I had a wonderful time. See you Friday."

Leon went home and there was a message on his machine. "Leon, Jack give me a call." "Okay." Leon dialed Jack's #, "Talk to me." "Hey Jack, it's Leon. What's up?" "Hey, where have you been?" "Oh, I couldn't wait for Friday to see Shondra so I went over this afternoon and we went for a walk." "Whoa dude, you have it bad." "I know. I can't help it. She's beautiful, sweet, kind, a joy to talk with and fun to be with, I just love everything about her." "Don't look now but it sounds like you're falling in love." "You mean like the way you feel about Lynetta?" "Yeah, that's what I mean." "I wonder how she feels about me?" "Has she said anything at all? Any kind of a hint?" "Well, when I called this afternoon she said she was thinking about me. And when I got to her door she opened the door before I could even knock on it." "Did she say any more?" Leon paused. "She did." "What did she say? Come on, I'm your best friend. You can tell me." "She said she missed me too." "She could be the one, Leon. You should take it slow. Don't rush things." "I know you're right but it's hard. Well I'd better get to bed. I'll talk to you later. Thanks for listening Jack." "Anytime, that's what friends are for. Goodnight."

At last Friday had arrived. In a few hours Leon and Jack would be taking their girls on their big date. Both Leon and Jack were getting ready for their dates. Lynetta and Shondra were each getting ready too. Finally, it was time. The guys left in Jack's car to pickup their dates. They picked up Lynetta first. "Hi We're going to get Shondra now." At Shondra's house Leon introduced everyone. "Jack, Lynetta, I'd like you to meet Shondra." Lynetta said, "Hi Shondra, it's nice to meet you." Jack said, "Yes it's nice to meet you." Then it's off to the restaurant.

At the restaurant Leon put them on the waiting list. "Well I put our names in so we're just waiting for our table." Soon the hostess called "Leon, party of 4" and they went in to dinner. They had a fabulous time at dinner. Then Leon asked, "So who's ready to go dancing?" Everyone smiled. "Okay, let's go."

It was a Friday night so the place was packed. "We may have to stand. I don't see any available tables or chairs for that matter." Just then a guy walked up to them and asked Jack, "Are you 4 looking for a table?" "Yes, we are. We didn't realize it would be this packed this early." "Well this is the early crowd. Some of us are getting ready to leave so you all can have our table if you want it." "Thank you, so much."

"Well I would hate to leave knowing I left two beautiful ladies standing all night when I could offer them a chair. You gents sure are lucky." "Well thank you." "Have a wonderful evening. Goodnight." "Goodnight." The four of them sat down at the table and listened to the music.

A slow song began and the guys asked the girls for a dance. So they all went to the floor and Leon asked, "Do you waltz?" Shondra said, "Sorry, no I can't." "Well would you like me to teach you how?" "Sure, but I'm not very good." "Relax. It's easy. Just follow my lead." Next thing she knew she was waltzing across the floor. Then the song ended. Leon told her, "See, I told you it was easy." "Wow. I did it!" "You sure did." he said with a big smile.

Jack and Lynetta came over and Jack said, "You two looked great together." Lynetta said, " Yeah, I didn't know you could waltz Leon." "Yeah, my mom taught me a few years ago. I'm surprised I remembered so well. I guess waltzing is one of those things that once you learn it, it comes right back. I just heard the music and instantly that's what my feet wanted to do. Plus having a beautiful lady to show off to everyone helps too." He winked at Shondra and she blushed.

The band came back on stage and asked whether everyone wanted a slow song or a fast one? The crowd hollered out, "S L O W!" So the band played a slow song and our two couples danced in the middle of the floor. As they moved to the rhythm of the music, Leon looked deep into Shondra's eyes. Slowly they leaned toward each other until they kissed. Lost in a kiss, they only stopped when the band began a fast song. Then Leon pulled away and looked at Shondra for a moment.

They both went back to their table and Leon said, "I've wanted to kiss you for so long now. I hope you didn't mind. I meant to..." She put her finger to his lips and quickly said, "I'm glad you did, I've wanted you to kiss me since our first date. You surprised me last time when you kissed my cheek but when I thought about it later I thought, how romantic, so I decided you were waiting for just the right moment." "Well, I was, kind of. I didn't want to rush it. To me a kiss means something special. It should say- I care a lot about you and this is how I want to show you." "I knew that somehow and I felt it when we kissed." "Come here baby."

Jack and Lynetta had gone to dance again so there were 2 empty chairs. Leon pulled one up next to him so when she sat down he could put his arm around her. They cuddled a bit, then she turned to look at him and they kissed again. They were both falling in love with each other and neither one wanted the night to end. Finally it was time to go. When they got to Shondra's Leon walked her to her door with his arm around her. At the door she said, "I wish you didn't have to go." "Me too. It'll seem like forever till I see you again." "I know." They kissed goodnight and she went inside.

Back at the car Jack said, "Leon, dude are you okay? Earth to Leon." He waved his hand in front of Leon's face, no response. Lynetta said, "Jack, it's a good thing you're driving. I don't think he's with us anymore." "I think you're right. Okay buddy, you just sit there and enjoy the ride." They took Leon home and by then he'd snapped out of it. "What, Where are we?" "You're home dude. You know what I think? I think you and Shondra are in love. I haven't seen that many sparks since the 4th of July."

"No kidding. That's how I feel when I look at her or even just think about her. She's..., she's..., I can't even describe her. She's everything I ever dreamed of, all in one woman. I can't believe it." "Calm down dude." "I can't." "Okay, well I'm going to take Lynetta home now. We'll talk tomorrow after we both get some sleep." "Okay dude, later. Goodnight Jack and thanks!" "Goodnight, you're welcome." Leon went in and went to bed but he couldn't go right to sleep. No matter which way he turned he could still see Shondra's face. Finally he fell asleep.

Once again he woke up with a smile on his face and hugging his pillow. As he laid there thinking of Shondra, his phone rang. He got up to answer it, "Hello?" "Hi Leon, It's Adrianne." "Oh hi, how are you? I'm sorry I haven't called. I've been kind of busy."

"I know, with your new girlfriend. By the way, how is Shondra?" "Huh, but how'd you...Lynetta." "Yep. What? You didn't think I'd find out?" "I shouldn't have tried to keep it a secret from you. I'm sorry Dre. Will you forgive me?" "It's okay. I forgive you." "Hey, wanna go for some coffee this morning? My treat, it...is still morning isn't it?" "I'd love to and yes Leon, it is still morning." "Shall we meet at our favorite coffee shoppe?" "Sounds great. Half and hour okay with you?" "Sure. I'll take a quick shower and meet you there." "Okay. See you soon. Bye." "See ya." They both hung up and got ready.

At the coffee shoppe they both arrived at the same time, so they went in together. They ordered and went over and sat on the corner couch. Adrianne began, "So, tell me all about her," she said, excitedly.

Leon started, "Well to begin with she's kind of shy, she likes to dance and last night I taught her how to, now don't laugh...waltz." Adrianne looked surprised and said, "Waltz? You know how to waltz?" "Yes. I know how to waltz. My mom taught me a few years ago." "Well you're just full of surprises." He crossed his arms across his chest, leaned back and said, "Alright, go ahead, have your fun." "No. I'm only teasing I think that's really cool." "You really think so?" "Yes I really do." "Oh Dre, I want you to meet her. I want all my closest friends to meet and get to know her and her to know all of you. I think of her everyday, every minute. When I wake up I can see her face. It's like she's right there in the room." "Wait, wait a minute, slow down, where's the fire?" "It's in my heart Dre." "Wow, you have it bad for her. Wait a minute, you're in love with her." "I guess I am? I've never really felt like this before. Oh Dre, do you think I could really be in love, with her?" "Yes Leon, I do." "And?" "I'm happy for you and I would love to meet her. She must be someone very special to make you feel this intense just after you two met." "She is! She's so wonderful I almost can't believe it myself. And beautiful, she's gorgeous."

Just at that moment Shondra and her 2 best friends were coming into the coffee shoppe. As Leon and Adrianne stood up he gave Adrianne a huge hug and a kiss (on the cheek) and said, "Thank you Dre. I love you." Shondra was shocked by what she just saw and heard. They all looked at Leon and Adrianne. Then Shondra's friends looked back at her as she shouted out, "NO!" and ran out the door. Rachel followed her.

Leon turned just in time to see Shondra running out the door in tears and started after her, but her friend Salena stopped him, "Whoa, boy! Just where do you think you're going?"

He said to Salena, "She doesn't understand." Salena said, "Then start explaining it to me, and it better be good." "Adrianne is a close friend of mine." "Oh sure, and you were just showing her your, what, brotherly love? Yeah like we haven't heard that one before." "No. You've got it all wrong! It's not what it looked like, really! I *have* to go after her!" He pulled free and ran out the door just in time to see her speed off in her car and Rachel was coming back. He yelled out, "Shondra!" But she kept going. Then he turned and went back in. He looked over at Adrianne with a devastated look and she said, "<u>Go</u> <u>after</u> <u>her</u>!"

So Leon ran out to his car, jumped in and peeled out after her. He drove around the area but he didn't see her car so he went to her house. When he saw her car there, he jumped out and raced up the steps. He pounded on the door and called her name over and over again. "Shondra please let me in. Let me explain what you saw. It's not what you're thinking. Please Shondra, please let me in. I Love You. You're the only one I want. Please believe me. Adrianne is just a very close friend and I was telling her all about *you* and how I feel about you. Please, don't shut me out. Tell me that you believe me?"

He heard a click on the other side of the door so he knocked and turned the doorknob and the door opened. He walked in, cautiously. He heard someone sobbing and went toward the sound. In the living room Shondra was laying on the couch crying. He rushed over to her. "Oh baby don't cry, I love you. You're the best thing that's ever happened to me. I just had to tell my friend Adrianne all about you. See, I've never felt like this about anyone before and I wasn't sure what I was feeling, so I talked to Adrianne and she told me that I'm in love with you. What you saw tonight was only 2 friends hugging, that's all."

Shondra sat up and said, "But you kissed her on the lips." "No. I kissed her cheek. and it was <u>just</u> a friendship kiss nothing more. Believe me." "I want to but..." "You can! If you want to you can even ask Adrianne. Shondra, I Love <u>you</u>. I know that now." "But..." Suddenly Leon kissed her passionately. "I couldn't kiss you like that if I didn't love you so much. I'm sorry I hurt you, but I thought you knew what my relationship with Adrianne was. She and I did date a few months ago but we're just friends now." "Are you sure you don't want to date her again?" "Yes. I'm very sure. What do I have to do to convince you? You are the only girl I want." (He paused a moment to think, then he said with a bit of saddness in his voice,) "But, maybe it isn't me. Maybe <u>you</u> don't love <u>me</u>? I know. I moved too fast didn't I and I blew it, right?" Leon got up to leave and with the sadness still in his voice he said, "I'm sorry I hurt you. I should go now. I won't bother you any more."

She reached out and stopped him from leaving. He turned to look at her once more as a tear ran down his cheek. She softly said, "No Leon. You're wrong. I *do* love you. That's why it hurt so much. I was just afraid to admit it to myself or to you but I can't deny it now. And I can say it now. I Love You! I love you more than I've ever loved anyone. Please, don't leave."

Leon looked over at her and as she brushed his tear away she said, "Now I'm sorry, I hurt you. Leon, please stay with me." "Are you sure?" "Yes. I'm sure." They leaned toward each other and kissed, a long and passionate kiss. They sat on the couch and cuddled together. Leon told her again, "I Love You." She replied, "I Love You too." As they sat there cuddled up, there was a voice at the door, "Shondra? Shondra?"

Shondra's friends walked in and saw Leon and Shondra in each others arms. Now the girls were all confused. "What?" They gasped. Shondra said, "It's all straightened out now. We're good." Rachel said, "But I thought..., weren't you, (she points to Leon) and Adrianne... you know?" Leon said, "No. We weren't. She just happens to be one of my best friends and I was telling her all about Shondra, that's all."

"Whew, that's a relief." Rachel said. "So everything 's okay?" Salena wasn't quite convinced and said, "Wait just a minute. You're not buying this story of his, are you Shondra?" Shondra looked up at Leon and said, "What do you think?" Then she and Leon kissed again. Salena said, "Okay we get it. But if you hurt her again, you're gonna have to deal with me." "Yes ma'am." Leon smiled. "Well, we'll leave you two alone now." Leon jumped up and said, "No, wait. Let's all go do something together so we can all get to know each other." Shondra said, "Great idea. And Leon, you go call Adrianne and why not Jack and Lynetta too." Rachel said, "Hey lets have a party."

Everybody said, "Yeah, a party." So Leon called everybody up and in a couple of hours the party was in full swing. There was food, soda pop, music and lots of fun between new friends and old all getting to know each other.

Now *there's* a happy ending! OR, Is it just the beginning...?

# Nine

## Lynetta's Discovery

Lynetta and Adrianne were hanging out with Alyssa at her place. Suddenly Lynetta got an idea and stood up. Dre said, "What's up ?" "I think I'll go shopping." "Now?" "Yeah, I just remembered, yesterday I saw the cutest pair of shoes in a store window but I didn't have time to go in to try on any. So I thought I'd go back today, when I'd have time to try them on and maybe buy them. See you girls later." Both Alyssa and Adrianne said goodbye.

Lynetta went down to the store but the shoes she wanted were gone. She went inside to see if they had any more. "Well Miss Hagen that's quite a popular shoe. We'll have to order a pair for you. What size do you need?" She ordered the shoes, said thank you and left. As she passed the other stores windows she admired all the displays.

Suddenly she heard: "Look it's Lynetta Hagen in front of that shoe store." "Are you sure?" "Sure as I'm standing here. I'm going to go get her autograph!" "Well let's go. Hurry up, before she leaves." Lynetta heard the word autograph and turned to greet her fans but when she turned around and saw a huge mob of paparazzi she got spooked. Being without any kind of security she ran away, frightened. She headed down the first ally she saw. Down the ally a bit she saw a large box and jumped behind it to hide. Her heart was pounding so hard she hoped nobody could hear it and find her. She heard, "Lynetta, Lynetta, we just want your autograph, please?" Normally she loved signing autographs for people but not like this. Large crowds like this can be brutal. She heard the crowd rush past and head on down the ally. When she was sure they were gone she came out and headed back the way she came. But she heard them coming back and started running again.

A security guard saw her running but didn't recognize her. He said, "Whoa Miss," as he grabbed her arm and pulled her aside, (thinking she was up to no good), "Wait just a minute. Where are you going in such a hurry?" Lynetta, looking worried said, "I have to hide or get out of here, please!" "Why? What did you do, rob someone or something?" "No, I'm Lyn..." She heard them getting closer and broke away from him.

She saw a door behind them and ran for it. She dashed through it just before the crowd, (now twice as large), rushed by. The security guard ran after her hollering, "You can't go in there, come back here." She went through the door and appeared to be in a back hallway. She saw another door and heard a noise coming through it so she went and opened the door to take a peek.

It appeared to be a large commercial kitchen that was very busy, so she sneaked inside and while she was looking for another exit a good looking young man appeared and said, "Can I help you?" "Do you have a side entrance I can use quickly?" "Sure, over there." He pointed to a door and opened it for her.

The security guard that was following her rushed into the kitchen knocking one of the kitchen staff into a large rack of pans which came crashing down making a deafening noise. Lyn said in a worried voice, "Oh no!" Everyone turned around to look at what the noise was all about. Before the guard could get to his feet and before Lynetta could run out the door, the young man grabbed her arm and pulled her back. She let out a gasp and looked at him with fear. Then she saw his finger pressed against his lips to say shh. He pointed to a big box standing in the corner where she could hide. Lynetta looked over and saw the guard getting up. She turned back around and the young man winked at her and nodded toward the box with a smile. So she hid behind the box just in time.

The guy pretended to be working when the guard came over. He saw the open door and heard the screen door slam. The guard ran out the door believing he was chasing Lynetta. The young man hurried over and closed the inside door, it locked when it closed.

He went over to Lynetta and said, "Coast is clear. You can come out now." She came out of hiding and said, "How can I ever thank you?" "Aw that's okay. You looked like you needed some help the way you came rushing in here." After she had time to take a good look at her hero she had a look of surprise and said, "Did anyone ever tell you that you look a lot like Jack Zachry?"

He gave a shy kind of smile, looked down at the floor and softly answered, "Yes, I get that a lot." She put her hand out and said, "Hi. I'm Lynetta..." "I know. It's nice to meet you. My name is Jeffrey Zachary, uh, no jokes please. I've heard them all." "That's your real name?" "Yeah, it is. I don't see the resemblance but everyone else seems to." "So what's your middle name?" "Allen." "So your initials are..." "Yes, they spell J.A.Z. My mom was into R & B and Jazz when I was born." He looked around as if looking for someone. Lynetta said, "Sorry, I ought to let you get back to work." "Well I do have a break coming up if you'd like to sit and talk a bit. But you probably have to get back to your boyfriend." "I have a few minutes for my hero." She smiled.

Jeffery gave her a shy smile and lead her to a back room with a small table for two where they could have some privacy. (Lyn was starting to get some people pointing at her and whispering.) "Would you like a soda or some water to drink?" "A soda would be fine." She asked, "What do you do for hobbies?" "Well I like to sing." "Have you ever performed on stage?" "Only if you count standing in front of my mirror with a brush or comb for a microphone." "It's a start." "Actually I used to record the songs I'd sing on a small recorder in my room. One time a friend found my tapes and took the few I had to a studio and had them made into demos." "Really? What happened?" "Nothing." "What do you mean?" "When I found out I got angry and when I got them back I stuffed them in my closet and there they still sit." "And your friend?" "I cooled off after he apologized. We're still friends." "I'd like to hear your songs sometime." "I don't know, I never did anything with them because I never thought they were very good." "I still would like to hear them or at least one of them." "Well, I keep my favorite one here in my locker. I'll let you borrow it if you really want to listen to it." "Yes I would." "Okay, I'll go get it, but remember, it probably isn't very good. I like it for the tune and the message. It means a lot to me. I'll be right back."

He came back with his CD and gave it to Lynetta to listen to. "Thanks Jeffrey. I can bring it back tomorrow." "That's fine. I'll be here." "See you about 1:00?" "Okay, that's about it for my break time. See you tomorrow. Right now, I'd better get back to work, while I still have a job." "Yeah, I'd better go too. So, see you tomorrow." "Yeah, tomorrow. Here I'll walk you out." Jeffrey walked her to the door and they said goodbye. Lynetta looked around for the paparazzi and left when she saw it was all clear.

At home she put in the CD Jeffrey gave her and sat down to listen. As the CD played she looked at the speaker in disbelief. By the end of the song tears were streaming down her face. Her CD player was set on repeat so as she sat there the song began again. Before the song ended again someone knocked on her door. She grabbed a tissue and answered the door. It was Alyssa. Lyssa saw her crying and said, What's wrong?" Lyn motioned to her, to come in and then closed the door behind her." After she cleared the lump from her throat Lynetta said, "Nothing's wrong. Come here. You have to hear this."

They entered the room just as the song was starting over and Lyn said, "Sit and listen." By the end of the song both girls were crying and Lyn got up to turn it off. Alyssa said, "WHO was that?" "His name is, get this, Jeffrey Zachary." (Lyn smiled.) "You're kidding." "No. And check out his middle name, Allen." "His name is Jeffery Allen Zachary?" "Right. J.A.Z. for short." "How did you meet him?" "I went to get those shoes earlier, remember? Well I was down at the shoe store..., Lynetta told Alyssa everything up to when Alyssa came to the door."

"Does he really look like Jack?" "Yes, a little younger than he looks now, but even I had to look twice." "And he sings like that. Wow. What are you going to do with the CD? And don't say give it back. I mean before you give it back. I know you too well." "I'm going to have my agent listen to it." "Don't you think Jeffrey should be in on it?" "Oh he will be. He just won't know it. Lyn smiled and went to the phone. "Who are you calling?" "You'll see. Put the song on again. Hi, Janet? It's Lynetta. I have a question for you. Oh, hold on I have to go get the paper I wrote it on, just a minute." Lynetta put the receiver down by the speaker and let Janet listen to a verse and a chorus then she picked up the phone again, "I'm sorry Janet, I'll have to call you back I can't find it." "Lynetta, who are you listening to? I don't recognize the voice or the song." "Oh, nobody, really. Just someone who likes to sing." "Does he have a label or an agent?" "No, I don't think so." "I'd like to meet this young man. Can you set it up?" "I think so." "I have some free time tomorrow night around 6:00. Is that enough time?" "I'll try. If I can't I'll call you by 3:00." "Good enough. Bye now."

"Okay I see those wheels turning. What are you up to?" "Oh nothing much. Let's just say I'm giving someone a helping hand." "You're going to have Jeffrey meet your agent aren't you?" "Maybe." "Maybe, *if* you can get him to come over here. How are you gonna do that?" "Well, you're gonna help." "ME? How am I gonna help?" "Well, for starters, you and I are going to have lunch tomorrow and that's all I'm going to tell you." "Okay, what time is lunch?" "Be here by 12:30 and we'll have plenty of time." "Okay, 12:30 it is. I have to go now. See you tomorrow. Bye." "Bye Lyssa, see you tomorrow."

Lynetta listened to the song one more time and once again it made her cry. As she got up to turn it off the phone rang and she answered it, "(sniffle) Hello?" "Hi Babe." "Oh, hi Jack." (he heard the sniffle) "What's wrong baby?" "Oh nothing." "Do you need me to come over?" "Oh I was just listening to a sad song, that's all. But you can come over if you want to." "I miss you. I'd like to see you, but if you're too busy..." "Okay, come on over." "See you soon." "Bye." They hung up and in a few minutes there was a knock on the door. Lynetta opened the door with a look of surprise. "What? Where did you call from, your car?" "Well, yeah." "You were on your way over here weren't you?" "Yeah. I can't help it. I wanted to see you." "I love you." "I'm glad cause I love you so much." He took her in his arms and kissed her. Then he picked her up and carried her to the couch and sat down with her on his lap.

Suddenly Jeffrey's song began to play. She tried to get up to turn it off but Jack only held on tighter. She said, "Let me up." "Why?" "I have to turn off the CD player." "Why? Let's hear it." The song played through and she cried again. "So that's the song that made you cry earlier? Who sings it?" "Some new guy." "Wow he's good. What label is he on?" "None." "None?" "A friend of his found his recording and had a demo made without his knowledge and he got mad so he stuffed it in his closet." "Is this a friend of yours?" "Not really." "So how 'd you get it?" Lyn explained to Jack what happened, "...And that's how I have the CD."

"You be careful around the paparazzi. Some of them can be brutal." "Yeah but thanks to Jeffrey I managed to escape." "Don't you mean the security guard?" "I don't know, he may have been one of the paparazzi *posing* as a security guard. Anyway I got away." "Still, you be careful. I don't want my girl getting hurt. So, do you get to keep the CD?"

"No. I'm giving it back tomorrow." "Do you want me to go with you?" "Uh, no. I'll just drop it off cause I'm going shopping with Alyssa tomorrow." "Okay, as long as someone I trust will be with you I'll feel much better." "Alright. You worry too much you know that?" "Can't help it. I'm in love with you and I don't want anything bad to happen to you." KISS......"Oh you. (Lyn smiled) Now go on home cause I'm going to bed early tonight. It's been quite a day for me and I'm rather tired. I'll see you later Goodnight Jack. Sweet dreams." "I'm going. Call you tomorrow?" "Sure, TOMORROW!" "Goodnight baby." They kissed goodnight and Jack went home.

The next day Alyssa showed up promptly at 12:30. "Here I am. Ready?" "Ready! Let's go." They got into Lynetta's car and took off. They parked near Jeffrey's workplace and walked on over. Alyssa said, "I can't wait to see this guy." "Now Lyssa, get a grip. Remember Jarrod, your boyfriend!" "Okay, I know, I know. I'll be cool."

They got to the kitchen, where Jeffrey works, and went in. Lynetta asked for Jeffrey Zachary and he came over. "Hi. I just punched out for lunch. Want to grab a bite? It's on me. And who's your cute friend?" "Alyssa this is Jeffrey, Jeffrey, Alyssa." "Hi, nice to meet you Jeff." She put her hand out to shake. He kissed the back of her hand and said, "It's nice to meet you. Okay who's hungry?" Lyssa said, "Me." Lyn said, "Oh twist my arm." "Let's go." He put both elbows out. Each girl took one and off they went to lunch. "Lynetta said, "You don't have to take us to lunch. I was just going to drop off your CD." "I know but I don't often get a chance to take one pretty lady to lunch let alone two. So allow me the pleasure, please?" "Well...since you put it that way. She looked at Lyssa nodding her head excitedly. Okay." "I know just where to take you lovely ladies." They walked down the street and there on the corner was a small cafe with an outdoor patio.

"Oh, this is nice" said Alyssa. "Yeah, I didn't know this was even here," added Lynetta. Jeffrey said, "I discovered it when I was looking for a different place to eat one day. So shall we?" Both girls said, "Yes."

So they went in, found a table and had a wonderful lunch on the patio. Soon Jeffrey's lunch hour was almost over. "Well I'm sorry ladies but this workin' man has to go back to work. But I don't remember a better lunch break. Thank you." Alyssa said, "Thank you." "Shall we go?" he said. And out the door they went.

They got back to his workplace and Lynetta started to look for his CD in her purse. "Ah here it is. Oh, wait. Let me make sure..." She opened the case, "Oh no, I don't believe it. I must have left it in my CD player. I played it several times last night and I thought I had put it back in the case. I should have checked this morning. I'm sorry."

Alyssa began, "We could bring- ow..." Lyn sharply jabbed her in the side with a smile. Lynetta said, quickly, "Jeffrey when do you get off work?" "About 5:00." "Okay, do you have plans for tonight?" "No. Just going home to shower, grab a quick bite and relax before bedtime. Why?" "Would you like to come over to my house for dinner? Then I can give your CD back to you tonight."

"Sounds great. What time shall I come over?" "6:00?" "Alright six it is. I'll run home, take a quick shower and come on over. There's only one small problem." "What?" "Where do you live?" "Oh, I guess you do need to know that. Here, I'll give you directions." Lyn wrote down the directions to her house along with her phone number and handed it to him. He took a quick look at it. "Okay, see you at 6:00. Say, is Alyssa going to be there?" Lyn asked, "Lyssa, are you coming over tonight?" "Sure, I'll be there." "Cool. Until tonight ladies." He bowed to the ladies and went back to work. That afternoon seemed to take forever to pass. Jeffrey kept looking at the clock and saying, "Come on clock, move."

Alyssa was like a giggly schoolgirl. "Oh my gosh, he is sooo cute." "Now Alyssa, don't forget, you're dating Jarrod. Remember? Jarrod? Your boyfriend? I can tell Jeffrey likes you but you have a boyfriend, don't you? You and Jarrod didn't...?" "Oh. No. We're still dating. It's just, I couldn't believe it the first time I saw Jack, how cute he was, and now there are <u>two</u> of them. Don't worry. I'll be fine."

The girls both got out at Lynetta's. Alyssa said, "See you tonight Lyn I'm going to go home and take a nap. I'll be back at six." "Okay Lyssa, see you later." Lyn went in and spruced up the house and got dinner started. Then she got ready for her guests and put dinner in the oven.

Meanwhile, Alyssa, instead of a nap, got a complete makeover. She called a hair stylist, makeup person and even got a manicure. It was almost 5:30. Time to leave for Lynetta's. Alyssa headed for her car just as Jarrod pulled up and parked. He got out and saw Alyssa all dressed up, like for a date. She was only thinking of one person and it *wasn't* Jarrod. She got in her car and took off for Lynetta's. She never even saw Jarrod. Jarrod was curious so he followed her. He'd been out of town all week on a shoot, so she was not expecting him. He came back early to surprise her. But he got the surprise.

"It's 5:55, whew, I have 5 minutes." She went to Lyn's front door and knocked. Lynetta answered it. "Alyssa? Is that you?" "Yes, it's me." "Wow, you look...different. I thought you were going to eat here with us? Is Jarrod back in town?" "No. I am eating here." "Lyssa aren't you a bit overdressed for lasagna?" "No, I don't think so." "Come on Alyssa. What would you say if Jarrod just happened to see you like this?" "I was waiting for you honey?" "Even though he's been out of town all week? Come on let's fix this. I think I have something you can wear and tone down the makeup. This isn't a movie."

"Okay so I went a little crazy." "A little?" "Okay a lot. But Jarrod's been gone so long and he hasn't called and I just miss him so much. Then Jeffrey seemed interested in me and well I guess I just lost my head." "Well here, fix your makeup and put this on and comb your hair down." "Not my hair." "Yes Alyssa, your hair." Lynetta handed her a comb as Alyssa closed the bedroom door.

Jarrod sat in his car trying to decide what to do when Jeffrey showed up. Jeffrey went to Lyn's door and knocked. Lynetta answered and let him in. A few minutes later Lyn's agent Janet showed up. Knock, knock. A voice yelled, "Come in!" Janet went in. Jarrod scratched his head. "What's going on?"

Alyssa came out of the bedroom looking more like herself and less like a movie star. But she still took Jeffrey's breath away. "Wow, Alyssa you look gorgeous." "Thanks Jeffrey."

Lynetta announced, "Dinner is almost ready. It will be just a couple more minutes. Oh, Jeffrey, this is Adrianne. Adrianne, Jeffrey." "A pleasure to meet you Adrianne." He kissed her hand. Adrianne replied, "And you as well Jeffrey." "And this is Janet." "Hello." "Hi Jeffrey." Lynetta asked, "Jeffrey, can I hear your CD once more before I give it back?" "I don't know. With all these people here?" "But they're just my friends, my closest friends. Please?" "Okay you can play it. Lynetta put in the CD and everyone sat down to listen. Jeffrey sat by Alyssa and put his arm over behind her. When the song began his arm curled around her shoulders. At the song's end Alyssa turned to look at Jeffrey and tell him what she thought of the song. But her face was so close to his that she forgot what she was going to say and she couldn't take her eyes off of him. Jeffrey leaned over to kiss her, when suddenly Lynetta said, "Well who's hungry?" That snapped Alyssa and Jeffrey back to reality. Jeffrey said, "Shall we go eat?" Alyssa said, "Sure."

As they all went into eat in the dinning room everyone was talking about the CD and how beautiful a song and how well done it was, then they were asking who the artist was? Finally Lynetta said to Jeffrey, "Go on, tell them who it is." Adrianne spoke up. "Okay Lyn, since you seem to know who the mystery artist is, tell us. Who sang that incredible song with that awesome voice." Lynetta looked at Jeffrey and all he could say was, "I did." Everyone around the table was so surprised they said, "You?" or let out a gasp. He said, "Yes, it was me. I wrote and recorded that song a couple of years ago." Alyssa and Adrianne asked to hear it again but Alyssa asked Jeffrey to sing along with the CD this time. "Please, for me?" she said. "Okay, for you Alyssa."

All this time Jarrod had decided to go for a drive, remembering the last time he and Alyssa had a misunderstanding. They almost broke up over it. He finally decided to get the guys opinions first. He drove to Jack's apartment since they usually hung out there. Sure enough there they were. Jack, Leon and Brian. He knocked. Someone shouted, "Come in." He walked in, "Hi guys." Jack said, "Hey Jarrod, when did you get back?" "Oh, awhile ago." "How was it out there? I'll bet the girls were <u>all</u> over you." "Oh there were a few but security was pretty tight. Say has anyone seen Lyssa lately?" "No. She's been spending time with Lynetta and Adrianne." "Has she mentioned me at all, since I left?" Leon, Jack, Brian?, "No not to me." "Not to me." "Nor me." "Well I think I'll go for a drive. See you guys later." Jarrod went back to the car. The guys all looked at each other. Leon said, now that was weird?"

Jarrod drove back to Lynetta's. "This time I have to find out what's going on in there!" He went to the door and heard music playing. Jeffery was singing with the CD to Alyssa and Adrianne. Just as Jeffrey reached for Adrianne's hand Jarrod quickly opened the door and everyone turned to see Jarrod in the doorway. Alyssa looked up and when she saw Jarrod she rushed over to him and hugged him and kissed him. Jeffrey finished the song and everyone applauded.

Lynetta's agent went up to Jeffrey and said, "Do you have an agent?" "No." "Would you like to have one?" "For what?" She turned to Lynetta, "Is he kidding?" " I'm afraid not. I didn't exactly tell him who you were, just that you're a friend." "You're sneaky. (she smiled) Let me introduce myself, I'm Janet Jones, Lynetta's agent and I'd like to be your agent if you're interested in a recording contract. Here's my card. My office and home number are on there if you're interested. If you are I'll look forward to hearing from you soon. I hope you'll call. I haven't heard a voice like yours in a long time and I'm positive you would do very well. I'll let you think it over. Goodnight everyone. And Lynetta, encourage him all you can. Goodnight." Lynetta said, "Okay, I'll do my best. Goodnight."

Jeffrey was standing with his arm around Adrianne but he was looking at Alyssa and Jarrod with a kind of sad look on his face. Adrianne was trying to encourage him to be a singer. Lynetta told him he should call her agent back and at least give singing a try. Just then Jarrod gave Alyssa a very passionate kiss. So suddenly, Jeffrey did the same with Adrianne. Adrianne was caught off guard and Jeffery asked, "Adrianne, can I take you home malady?" "Sure." "Let me just say goodnight to everyone first." Jeffrey told everyone goodnight and escorted Adrianne to the car. "Would you like to go for a cup of coffee or something?" "Coffee sounds great."

"You...don't happen to have a boyfriend...do you?" "Oh, no. Leon and I dated a few times but we're just friends now and I'm not seeing anyone right now." "Is Jarrod Alyssa's steady boyfriend?" "Yeah. They've been going out a couple of years now. They met at the studio and really hit it off." "So where has Jarrod been all week?" "Oh he was out of town on a shoot. He came back early to surprise Alyssa I guess." "You guess?" "Yeah, he wasn't due back until Sunday night. I guess he missed Alyssa that much and it looks like she missed him too." They went to have some coffee and get to know each other.

As the night wore on they talked about a lot of things, then the conversation seemed to die down and Adrianne noticed Jeffery folding and unfolding a napkin like a nervous habit, so she calmly put her hand on his and he looked at her. Then she quietly said, "It's Alyssa and Jarrod isn't it?" He looked surprised. But looking at her face, he could tell, she knew. The words wouldn't come so he looked down and nodded.

Adrianne said, "It's okay, I knew when you kissed me. You have a crush on Alyssa but she's in love with Jarrod." "Why didn't she tell me about him?" "You have to ask *her* that." "I feel like such a fool." "You're not a fool. But you are cute." She tried to get him to smile a little. They sat quietly for a little while. Each one looking up at the other and back down until they both looked at each other and she smiled at him. He reached up and ran his finger down her cheek. "I never noticed before just how beautiful you really are." Then he leaned over toward her and she toward him and they kissed.

"I should get you home young lady." "I guess so." Jeffrey took Adrianne home. "Would you like to go out with me again?" She said, "Yes, I'd like that." "Honest?" "Yes Jeffrey, honestly." "Okay I'll call you." "I hope so, even if we only go for coffee. I like spending time with you." "Thanks, same here." "Well, see you later." She turned to go in, "Adrianne?" She turned back to him, "Yes?" He kissed her again and said, "Goodnight beautiful and thanks for not being angry." She smiled and said, "You're welcome and goodnight." Then she turned and went inside.

Next morning Adrianne's phone was ringing. She answered, "Hello?" "Hi gorgeous." (She smiled) "Good morning Jeffrey." "I hope it's not too early to call, but would you like to go to breakfast with me?" "Sure, just give me half an hour and I'll be ready." "Is that enough time? I can give you an hour." "No, half an hour is fine." "Okay, see you then. Bye gorgeous." "Bye Jeffrey."

In half an hour Jeffrey was knocking on Adrianne's door. She answered, "Hi come on in, I'm almost ready." He opened the door and went in. Adrianne walked out of the bedroom, "Okay, I'm ready." He looked at her like something was missing and said, "No, not yet. But, maybe this will help?" Jeffrey pulled a long stemmed red rose from behind his back and gave it to her. Oh, it's beautiful. Thank you." "It's not half as pretty as you are. Now you're ready!" "Okay, let's go." So off they went to breakfast.

At the cafe Adrianne asked, so, are you going to sign a recording contract?" "I don't know. I never thought about singing for a living. I've always done it just for the fun of it. I think if I <u>had</u> to do it for a living, it just wouldn't be fun anymore. And performing in front of a lot of strangers. I just don't know. That's fine for the people who want to but I just don't think it's me and your life is always under a microscope. I couldn't do things like this just whenever I wanted. My life would be on a schedule." "I understand." "Do you?" "Believe me, I do."

There was an awkward silence between Adrianne and Jeffrey. Both wanted to say something to the other but were afraid. Then Jeffrey spoke first. "I'm not sure how to put this without it coming out wrong." "Okay just say it and then tell me what you meant to say." "Alright here it is. I want to... date you but I don't want to." "And what does that mean?" "I like you but I'm afraid with the whole Alyssa thing...I just don't want you to...well, I feel like I'm on the rebound and if we're going to have a relationship I want it to start out right. I want to start fresh. Do you know what I mean?" "I think so."

"I think I need a few days to sort out my feelings. If I ask you to, will you wait for me?" "Yes Jeffrey. If you're asking me to, I'll wait for you. Take the time you need but don't take too long." "Okay, but for now I should take you home."

Jeffrey took Adrianne home. He walked her to her door and she said, "I'll be waiting. Let me know what you decide? Goodbye for now. I'll miss you." "I hope I can give you the answer you want to hear. But not just now. I need some time alone. But I do think that I will miss you, too." He whispered in her ear, "Keep your fingers crossed." Then they kissed goodbye and he left.

# Ten
## Alyssa's Disappointment

It's 6:00 a.m. Time for rehearsal to begin. Danny had everyone lined up for warm-ups. Half and hour later the real work began. Before they all realized it rehearsal was over and it was time to go home. Alyssa was packing her stuff up then Danny said, "I need to see you before you leave." "Sure Danny."

Just before Alyssa left she went to Danny, "Hi Danny, what's up?" "I know you and your understudy Linda are pretty close, right?" "Yeah, we are. Why? Did something happen?" "Nothing bad. She just couldn't bring herself to tell you she had to take a leave of absence for awhile and she doesn't know for how long." "Why? What happened?" "She has a family member who's very ill and she needs to be there."

"But who's going to be my understudy now?" "We're going to start tryouts tomorrow. We'll start with callbacks of the ones who tried out before Linda was chosen." "Okay Danny. When does Linda have to leave?" "She's coming in tomorrow to say goodbye to everyone and plans to leave the end of the week, So, you'll have a little more time together before she leaves. And remember I'm here if you need a shoulder." "Thanks Danny. I just may need that." That night Alyssa went shopping to find just the right going away gift for Linda to remember her by.

The next morning Alyssa tried to get there early to surprise everyone, but Danny had a surprise himself. He had the whole room decorated with balloons and streamers and even a huge cake that said, "We'll Miss You! Hurry Back! Love, The Cast." When Alyssa saw that she started to cry. So Danny walked up to her and gave Alyssa a big bear hug and said "Don't cry now save it till later." So Alyssa put on a smile and when Linda walked in she was so surprised she was speechless.

Danny didn't really have rehearsal that day. He let everyone have the day to say goodbye to a good friend and to give and get phone numbers and addresses to keep in touch with Linda.

The rest of the week was hard to get through, especially for Alyssa but somehow she did it. Friday was finally here. The day Alyssa had been dreading but she was prepared for it or so she thought.

Linda came over to Alyssa's place one last time and gave Alyssa a picture of the two of them together. They both cried and said how much they would miss each other. Linda said, "I have to go. I love you Alyssa, I'll call you!" "I love you Linda." They hugged once more and Linda left. Alyssa sat and cried for a little while, then she got up and went to rehearsal. Danny *and* Alyssa's friends were so surprised to see her walk in. Danny said, "Alyssa you don't have to be here today. I know how hard Linda's leaving must be for you, so I didn't expect you to come in. Why don't you just take a long weekend?" "No. I need to do something. I need to keep busy." "Okay, if you're sure." "I am." "Alright. I'm glad you're here." Danny gave her a big hug and rehearsal began.

After rehearsal Alyssa's closest friends came over to let her know, if she needed anything she could count on them day or night. Lynetta said, "Lyssa would you like to come over to my place this weekend? I'm having an all girl sleepover." "No. I don't think so, I don't want to be a wet blanket. Thanks anyway." Lynetta nodded to Adrianne to encourage Alyssa to come over. "Oh come on Lyssa you know how much fun we girls have together, please say you'll come?"

Leon over heard the conversation and chimed in with, "Hey, sounds like fun can I come too?" Lynetta said, "No. It's girls only." "Oh, bummer. Why don't you go Lyssa? Sounds like it will be a blast." " I don't know. I don't want to ruin their fun." Jack was just close enough to hear what Leon and Alyssa both said and from the looks on Lynetta's and Adrianne's faces he figured out what they were trying to do so he stepped up and added, quietly, in almost a whisper, "Go on Alyssa, you know you'll have a great time. And if you don't go you know all the fun you're going to miss out on. Just remember the last sleepover you were at." Alyssa thought for a moment and a slight smile came to her face. Jack winked at Lynetta and gave her a nod so Lynetta asked once more, "Please come Lyssa?" Slowly she said, "Well okay, if you're all sure?" Everybody, (guys too) jumped up and shouted, "YEA!! Alright Alyssa."

Alyssa was so surprised at the response she could hardly believe it. "Okay since you got me to come what time shall I be there?" "I was thinking about 6:00 or whenever everyone can get there. I'll just play some music and stuff until everyone gets there. It's a sleepover not a formal dinner. Come as you are, stay as long as you want. See you all later."

The girls went on home to get ready for the sleepover. Jack got an idea. "Hey guys." He motioned to the guys to come over. "Wanna get together and have some fun tonight?" The guys all said "Yeah, sure." "Okay, meet at my place at 6:00." They all agreed. "See you guys later." said Jack.

At 6:00, the girls all showed up at "Lynetta's and the guys all showed up at Jack's. Jack let the guys in, then told them his plan. "So is everybody in?" They all agreed. Jack had given each guy a small task to do and then head over to Lynetta's house. The guys all finished quickly and now they were all in front of...Lynetta's house. Together they went up to the door and rang the bell. Lynetta answered the door but all she could see was flowers. Her response was, "What in the world, who...?" Then all of a sudden the flowers parted and she heard a loud, "SURPRISE!" Each one of the guys showed what they had brought. Brian brought flowers, Leon brought the soda, and Jack brought chocolates. Jack said, "We just wanted to help make sure you girls have a fun night tonight."

Just then a guy in a tux with a flashing bow tie showed up and asked, "Is there an Alyssa Tillman here?" "Sure, just a minute, Lyssa someone's here for you." "Who?" "You'll have to come and see." When Lyssa got to the door the guy in the tux gave her a balloon bouquet, then he pulled flowers from his sleeve, and last of all he sang her a "singing telegram" which ended, Love always, Jarrod.

Alyssa said to Lynetta "Oh please, let them come in for awhile? They made me so happy." "Okay, for awhile." The guys came in and stayed for hours. Finally Lynetta told all the guys, "Alright boys this has been great fun but it's time for you to go home now." Jack said, "Okay we're going. Do I get a goodbye kiss?" "Alright." Lynetta kissed Jack goodbye. Leon said to Dre, "And do I get one?" Dre said, "Okay, here." Then she kissed Leon. Brian just looked at the floor and kicked his foot when suddenly Alyssa walked over and gave Brian a great big hug and an even bigger kiss. Everybody looked at each other with a surprised look on their face then they looked back at Alyssa and Brian. Alyssa turned and saw them all looking at her in disbelief. "What? I just didn't want Brian to feel Left out." Everyone said, "Yeah. Sure. Right. We understand." The guys and girls said goodnight to each other and the guys left and went home.

The next morning at Lynetta's the girls were all up and dressed when Lyn heard the doorbell. She answered the door. Jack was standing there with 2 beautiful red roses and a big smile, "Good morning beautiful." He handed her the flowers while she stood there speechless then he escorted her inside.

The doorbell rang again and Jack said, "Hey Dre would you get the door please?" She said, "Sure." Adrianne opened the door and Leon was standing there with 2 carnations of her favorite color in his hand and a big smile, "Good morning, beautiful." He handed her the flowers and escorted her inside.

The doorbell rang once again and Leon said, "Hey Lyssa would you get the door please?" She said, "Sure, why not?" and she let out a small chuckle." She opened the door and Brian was standing there with 2 bright yellow roses and a big smile, "Good mornin' Miss Alyssa."he said, in his best southern gentleman imitation complete with a low bow at the waist as he presented the flowers to her. So she likewise made a curtsy and accepted them with a little *southern flavor* of her own, "Why thank you kind sir. Won't you please come into my parlor?" To which he replied, "How very kind of you. May I escort you little lady." "You certainly may." Alyssa proudly took his arm as they joined the others. Then as Alyssa sat down Brian finished his "part" by kissing the back of her hand.

Leon said, "Did we make a detour down *southern Alabama* way?" Then Brian and Alyssa started to laugh. And everyone had a good laugh.

Jack said, "How would you lovely ladies like us to take you to breakfast this fine morning?" The girls all looked at each other and nodded in agreement. "We'd love to." They all headed to their favorite cafe and had breakfast in the corner booth. With all six of them together Brian and Alyssa had to sit rather close together.

After breakfast the guys took the ladies back to Lyn's house. At the door the girls thanked the boys for breakfast and the boys said goodbye and left.

Jack said, "Hey guys wanna go shoot some hoops?" Brian said, "Why don't you two play one on one and I'll just watch." Jack asked, "Are you sure?" Leon asked, "You don't want to play?" Brian said, "I'm sure. I'd rather just sit and watch. <u>Really</u>." Brian sat down and started watching Jack and Leon play B-ball but before long his thoughts began to drift.

Soon he found himself remembering last night, bringing Alyssa the yellow roses and this morning when he got to sit so close to her at breakfast that he could smell her wonderful perfume. But he liked best, the way the corners of her mouth turned up when she smiled, and it made him smile too. He thought how wonderful it felt when she kissed him last night. Suddenly he thought, "I have to stop this. She's dating Jarrod. <u>We</u> are <u>just</u> friends."

Back with the girls, Alyssa was really missing Jarrod. Lynetta told her, "If you miss Jarrod so much call him and talk to him Lyssa." Dre said, "Yeah girlfriend, call the man." So Alyssa called Jarrod's cell phone... But when she did, instead of hearing Jarrod's voice, she heard a woman's voice answer with, "Hello. Jarrod's busy right now. You'll have to call back later. Bye." The phone then went right to his voice mail, but she hung up instead of leaving a message. Alyssa was shocked and started to cry. She began to imagine all kinds of things he could be doing.

Lynetta and Dre asked her, "What's wrong?" Alyssa finally calmed down enough to tell them, "A woman with a very sexy voice answered Jarrod's cell phone. His <u>private</u> number. He's with another woman." Lynetta said, "Are you sure? Maybe you dialed a wrong number." "<u>No.</u> She said Jarrod's busy right now you'll have to call back later. Then all of a sudden the phone went to his voice mail."

Lyn's phone rang, "Hello?" "Hi, it's Brian. Can I talk to Alyssa for a minute?" "I don't know. I'll ask. Alyssa, Brian wants to talk to you, shall

I tell him you're busy?" She shook her head and reached for the phone. "Hi Brian what's up?" "I just wanted to hear your voice again really. Is...everything alright? You sound different." "Oh you know those sappy movies and all." "Oh, well I don't want to bother you..." "You're not. I'm glad you called." "Really?" "Yeah." "Well I was thinking, since Jarrod is out of town, would you like to go for a walk, you know,as friends?" "Sure. That sounds great." " Is now a good time?" "Now is great. I'll be waiting for you. Bye Brian." "Bye Lyssa."

Lynetta and Adrianne looked at each other with a look of concern. One minute she's crying and the next she's smiling and happy? Lyn said, "Okay Lyssa what's going on?" "Nothing. A friend is coming over and we're going for a walk. That's all." "Who's coming over? Brian?" "Yes Brian." "Oh good, we can all go for a walk, right Dre?" "Right!"

"Wrong. Brian invited me, not the entire group. I don't need babysitters." "Alyssa it's not fair to use Brian to get back at Jarrod. Think of Brian's feelings. I think he likes you but he's holding back because of Jarrod, and I won't let you hurt him that way, even if it means we're not friends anymore." Dre said, "That goes double for me." "Well Brian and I are good friends and *we're* going for a walk, together." Lyn's doorbell rang. Alyssa answered, "Hi Brian." "Hi Alyssa, Lynetta, Dre. Alyssa, you ready?" "Yes, let's go."

Lyn said, "I'm going to find out what Alyssa heard." She looked through her phone numbers and at last she found Jarrod's cell phone number and called it. This is what she heard: (a woman's sexy voice saying), "Hello Jarrod's busy right now you'll have to call back later. B... hold on don't hang up. I'm here." Jarrod picked up. Lyn said, "Jarrod?" "Yeah it's me. Who's this?" "Lynetta. Who answered your phone?" "Oh that, it's a new message someone put on my phone as a joke. I'd better change it before Lyssa hears it. I've been so busy with the shooting schedule I just haven't had the time." "Uh, Jarrod, it's too late, that's why I'm calling." "What do you mean?" "Alyssa called your phone this morning and now..." "And now she thinks I'm with another woman. Do you know where she is now?" "Well, Brian came over and they went for a walk." "Well that seems harmless enough." "But Jarrod she was really hurt and I'm afraid she's going to hurt Brian by leading him on. Can't you come home, just for a little while?"

"I knew I should have changed that message sooner. Well I do have a couple of days off coming but they're split up. Maybe I can get them to move some things around, I'll see what I can do. When you see Lyssa please try to explain that my friends were playing a joke on me because I'm so far away from Alyssa and I talk about her all the time, I guess. Please let her know how much I love her." "Okay Jarrod just get here as fast as you can." "I will. Bye and Thanks." "You're welcome. Goodbye Jarrod."

Jarrod went to the director to ask for some time off so he could go home and straighten out things with Alyssa. But the Director said, "Sorry Jarrod, I don't have the time to give you right now. This shoot is already costing more money than I wanted it to. I've been trying to stay under budget but we're rapidly approaching the limit, if we haven't gone over already. I'm sorry your girlfriend is just going to have to understand. Or you'll have to try to fix it long distance. I can't even afford to replace you if you decide to walk out. Please let's just get this shoot done and we can <u>all</u> go home." "But she thinks I-" "Jarrod I'm sorry! My hands are tied. The answer is no! You'll have to do the best you can from here. That's it! Someone get me my script. I've misplaced it."

"Here you are sir. It was in the booth. Coffee sir?" "Yes please, and make it strong. Let's go people before we loose the light."

Jarrod sat down in his chair and tried to figure out how he was going to make Alyssa understand that his actor friends were just playing a practical joke on him. "Yeah right, what's practical about that joke?" Jarrod was slowly becoming angry over the whole joke prank now that he knew Alyssa had heard it and obviously assumed the worse. "I could just throttle Tina for being part of that and just because I wouldn't go out with her and her oddball friends the other night. Oh I'd love to get them back somehow. But that doesn't help me fix things with Alyssa now."

"Hi Jarrod honey." "Tina." "My friends and I are going out for drinks after work, wanna come with?" "No thanks. I have some stuff I have to do after work and I may not get finished before I have to turn in. Sorry. Thanks anyway." "Come on Jarrod, you know what they say about all work and no play...(she began tickling behind his ear). You need some time off to relax too. Come on. Say you'll go, please?! I promise to be good." "I can't, sorry. Besides I want to call Alyssa tonight. But you all have a good time tonight."

The director called, "Okay places everybody. Let's get as much done as we can before we wrap for today. Ready...and action-" They worked for four more hours then the director yelled, "CUT! That's a wrap for today. Let's pick it up right here tomorrow morning bright and early and see if we can get it finished tomorrow. Goodnight everybody."

As soon as everyone was dismissed Jarrod went to his dressing room and after a quick shower he called Alyssa. "Hello, this is Alyssa please leave a message after the beep.* BEEP" "Alyssa, don't hang up. Honey, it's Jarrod, I know you think I'm cheating on you but I'm not. The guys here got tired of me always talking about my wonderful girlfriend and they put one of the girls up to changing my message on my phone. I know I should have changed it as soon as I heard the message they left but I never thought you would hear it before I could. I've been so busy with the shoot I just haven't had the time to change it. I can't wait for this to be done and be on my way home to you baby. I miss you so much.

I even asked the director for time off to come and see you to straighten all this out but he said no. So for now I'm stuck here. Baby please don't do anything rash. I know you're spending time with Brian as a friend I only hope it isn't any more than that. If you want me to, I'll leave the shoot right now and come home to you. The director said he can't afford to replace me but if it's that important to you I'll do it. I only hope it doesn't come to that. I hope you can trust me to be faithful to you while we're apart. I love you Alyssa. Kisses and lots of hugs from me to you baby. Goodnight. (I hope she listens to all of that. I don't know what else to do or say.)"

Jarrod sat in his little room hoping and praying that Alyssa would call him back and tell him she understood and would wait for him to come home. He was kind of glad Brian was there for her but at the same time he was worried that in his absence she might just latch on to Brian and not let go. And poor Brian stuck right in the middle. "I know he likes Alyssa but he's honest to the core and would never come between Alyssa and I. Please Lord help me fix this huge misunderstanding. Amen."

It was getting later and later and still Alyssa hadn't called Jarrod back. He was beginning to wonder if she even listened to his message or if she might have just deleted it without listening to it. "Alyssa please call me! Please!" He laid on his bed and while waiting for her to call he fell asleep. Soon he began to dream.

He saw Alyssa dressed in her prettiest dress and looking so beautiful. She was patiently waiting on the couch for her man. There's a knock at the door. She slowly gets up to answer the door. She reaches out and turns the doorknob. Slowly the door opens. "Hello there." "Hello gorgeous. Ready to go?" "I'm always ready for you...Brian." He woke up, "WHAT? Brian?" "Oh no! I gotta do something, NOW!"

Jarrod picked up his phone and called Alyssa. Ringing... Hello, this is Alyssa. Please leave...BEEP. Alyssa it's Jarrod where are you baby? We need to talk please! Pick up the phone or call me back. I LOVE YOU! I REALLY DO! I'm begging you, please call me!"

Back with Alyssa and Brian, "Ha, ha, ha, oh Brian you are so funny. I just love spending time with you. You are so easy to talk to." "Isn't Jarrod easy to talk to?" "Oh let's not talk about him Brian." Suddenly Brian got very quiet. "Brian, are you alright?" "What makes you say that?" "You suddenly got very quiet." "So." "Are you...upset with me?" "Should I be?" "I don't think so." "Uh huh." "Brian, what did I do?" "Just answer me one question." "Okay." "Do you still love Jarrod?" Alyssa had a strange and puzzled look on her face, but she didn't answer him. Then he said, "That's it! I'm leaving!" "Brian?" "Look, until you can decide how you feel about Jarrod I'm not coming over any more. You have to face this Alyssa. Whether you make up or break up with <u>him</u>, until you do one or the other, we're done. Goodbye Alyssa." "Brian!"

Brian just turned and walked away without looking back. It was killing him to do that to her but it needed to be done if there was going to be any hope for them. He really wanted to tell her to just break up with him but he knew that was wrong. If Jarrod and Alyssa were going to break up it would have to be a decision between Jarrod and Alyssa only. He would have no part of that. Brian finally made it home.

Alyssa went home and thought about everything Brian had said. Then as she was walking by the phone she noticed she had 2 new messages. "I wonder who called?" She hit play, "Alyssa, don't hang up. Honey, it's Jarrod, I know you think I'm cheating on you but I'm not. The guys..." She almost deleted the message twice out of anger but after remembering what Brian had said to her she thought she ought to listen. After all there are two sides two every story and she had to admit she really hadn't given Jarrod a real chance to explain his side of it. Plus after hearing his velvety soft voice she began to soften a bit. Especially with the way he sounded like he was in a lot of pain. She listened to the first message all the way through. Then she listened to the second one. By the end of the second message Alyssa was in tears.

"What's wrong with me? How could I do that to someone who loves me so much? And how could I use Brian like that? It would serve me right if neither one wanted to talk to me ever again." She put her face in her hands and cried.

A few minutes later her phone rang. The caller ID said, Jarrod. Suddenly she was all thumbs as the answering machine began, "Hello, this is Alyssa-" Finally she picked up and answered her cell, "Hello, hello I'm here, don't hang up!" "Alyssa? Oh honey, it's so good to actually hear your voice. I'm so sorry for everything you went through. I feel like it's all my fault." "No, no, no, I just jumped to the wrong conclusions. I know you would never cheat on me. I don't know why I thought..." Her voice trailed off.

"Honey are you there?" She softly said, "Yes." "What is it baby?" "I...have a confession...to make." "What honey?" "I...went out...with Brian." "Oh honey, I'm glad you have such good friends to take care of you when I'm away." "But you don't understand. I...I was flirting with him and I feel so bad now. How could I do that to either one of you?" "Honey, you were hurt and angry and with good reason. You thought I was cheating on you and I don't blame you for feeling like that. I only hate myself for not erasing that stupid message sooner, so something like this wouldn't happen."

"But I didn't have to go running to Brian." "Maybe you did?" "What?" "You needed someone strong to take care of you when I couldn't. I'm just glad Brian was there for you. I'll have to thank him when I get back." "Uh, that...might not be such a good idea." "Why not?" "Because, I think Brian...likes me...a lot!" "Oh, I see. Well that makes him even more of a hero, knowing how he must feel about you and to not take advantage of you when I'm not there."

"Oh but Jarrod I really wasn't fair to him the way I threw myself at him." "Honey I'm sure he understands. It will be alright. I promise." "Well I should at least go apologize to him. I only hope he doesn't hate me." "Now who could possibly hate you? You do what you think you need to, to fix things. I trust you. I love you. I'll be home as soon as we finish." "I love you Jarrod. I'm so glad you understand. See you soon my love." "Bye sweetheart." They each blew a kiss before hanging up.

Alyssa swallowed hard and went to see Brian at his place. Brian kept thinking about Alyssa and Jarrod. Then he heard a knock on his front door and went to answer it. Alyssa timidly said, "Hi Brian. I know you probably don't want to see me right now but, I came...to apologize. I had no right to treat you like I did and I'm sorry. Are we... still friends?" He finally said it out loud, "Alyssa I need to know, did you and Jarrod break up or not?" The words hit Alyssa like a ton of bricks. She was stunned. She hadn't heard it put so bluntly before and she was suddenly at a loss for words. It was almost like some knocked all the wind out of her.

"Well Alyssa? I have to know before this goes any farther. I like you, probably more than I should. But I don't want to come between you and Jarrod." "Oh Brian, I'm sorry I led you on. I'm just glad you..." "Have good brakes?" "Yes." "But Alyssa, I do still care for you, a lot. I hate myself for thinking this, but...I was secretly hoping...that...Jarrod had fallen for one of those gorgeous California girls, then I...oh never mind. It was a stupid idea. If Jarrod makes you happy then so am I. BUT- If he <u>ever</u> hurts you he'll have to deal with me!" "My knight in shining armor. Thanks Brian."

At Brian's front door Alyssa reached up to kiss Brian's cheek and said, "Still friends?" He smiled and said, "Best friends!" They gave each other a big friendly hug and Alyssa turned to leave. Brian called out, "See you later...friend!" She turned and smiled giving him a wave as she headed back to Lynetta's house.

Lynetta looked up when Alyssa came in. "Are you okay Lyssa? Did you...?" Alyssa gave her half a smile and said, "Don't worry, everything is just fine. Brian and I are still friends. But I think our friendship is on a different level now, deeper maybe."

Not knowing about Jarrod's conversation with Alyssa Lyn said, "Lyssa, I know Jarrod still loves you and if you listen to your heart you will know it too." "Did he call you?" "As a matter of fact, yes he did and he explained <u>everything</u>." Just then her doorbell rang. Lyn went to answer it. In a minute she came back and said with a smile, "Alyssa, someone's at the door for you." "Who?" "Go find out."

Alyssa went to the door and opened it. When she looked up she saw 2 huge bouquets of the prettiest red roses ever. As the flowers parted she saw who was behind them. It was Jarrod. While Alyssa was standing there starring at Jarrod, trying to believe he was really there,

Dre and Lynetta came over and took the flowers from Jarrod and said, "We'll put these in some water." Suddenly Alyssa ran up to Jarrod and began hugging and kissing him over and over again. When she finally settled down Jarrod explained about how he got the time off to come home and see her. He still hadn't changed the message on his phone. He handed it to her as they sat on the couch and he said to her, "Lyssa, sweetie, I'm going to change the message on my phone and honey, I want <u>your</u> voice to be the one to leave the <u>new</u> message on my cell phone." Alyssa smiled. She left this message: "Hello, Jarrod is <u>un</u>-available but you may leave a message after the tone. Goodbye."

Jarrod took Alyssa out to dinner that night. He told her, Alyssa, please, never doubt my love for you. There isn't anyone in my heart but you. Please believe me. I Love You! I believe I always will. Now, how are things between you and Brian now?" "Much better thank you, but I'd better warn you, you'd better be very careful cause if you ever hurt me, Brian said you'll have to deal with him." "Looks like I don't have to  worry about you any more. You have you're very own bodyguard." Alyssa just smiled.

She kept on smiling and Jarrod said, "What?" She thought a moment and said "Oh nothing, <u>really</u>..." "Lyssa, no secrets, remember?" "I know. I was just thinking, I have the greatest friends in the world." "How do you mean?" Alyssa told him about Linda leaving and how upset she was. Then she told about everything her friends did to cheer her up. Up to and including her walk with Brian.

"Okay Jarrod you said- 'no secrets' so here goes, you know I was flirting with Brian <u>after</u> I heard your phone message. But, Brian said he didn't want to come between us because he knew how much I still loved you and that I was acting out of anger and pain. End of story." "I'm so sorry Lyssa. It's all my fault for not erasing that stupid message Tina left. I knew about the phone message and I should have at least erased it right away and then you never would have heard it and gotten so upset."

"It's alright Jarrod. I knew you would never cheat on me but when I heard another woman's voice on your private phone all sense of logic left me. I wish I wouldn't get so jealous. It's just that you're so good looking and with all the pretty girls that must throw themselves at you when I'm not there, the temptation must be enormous." "But Alyssa the difference between you and them is I know you and I <u>love</u> you.

They may be pretty, but, I need more than that and you give me both. Also you have something that none of them ever will." "What?" "You have my heart! Hook, line and sinker." They had been sitting on the couch all this time, so Jarrod stood up in front of Alyssa, pulled something from his pocket, then he knelt on one knee. Then looking into Alyssa's eyes he took her left hand in his and said, "Alyssa, as long as you'll have me I promise to love you with my whole heart and soul. It's like you're the other half of me. Will you marry me?" He started to put the ring on her finger and held it there until she gave him her answer. "Yes Jarrod. I'd love to marry you. And I promise to be true to you as long as we're together. I love you Jarrod." Jarrod pushed the ring completely on her finger, a perfect fit. "I love you Alyssa." And they sealed their promises with a very passionate kiss. Lynetta and Adrianne both expressed their heart felt joy for both of them.

# Eleven

# The Big Misunderstanding

Today is so picturesque that looking out the window is just like looking at a photograph. Snow has covered the ground like a soft, glittery, white blanket. And everything else looks like it was dusted with powdered sugar, all billowy and soft. In Lynetta's front yard there stood a giant, round, white snowball.

As Lynetta stood there with her hot cocoa, looking out at everything, her phone rang, "Hello?" "Hi baby. What's my girl doing this beautiful winter morning?" She sighed and said, "Just looking out my window at my winter wonderland." "Well shall I come over so we can finish Mr. Snowman?" "Sure. Come on over and I'll fix you some hot cocoa." "Awesome I'll be right over."

A few minutes later Jack arrived at the door. Knock, knock. "Come in." He came in and when he didn't see Lynetta he said, "Okay where's my baby?" She called out, "In the kitchen." Jack went to the kitchen just as Lyn was stirring his hot cocoa. "Good morning doll." "Good morning." -Kiss- Hug- then she handed the hot cocoa to him. "Oh thanks. It is cold out there." "Then we should bundle up if we're going to go finish Mr. Snowman." Lynetta went to get her coat, gloves and scarf. After she put her coat on Jack took her scarf and carefully wrapped it around her. He gave her a big kiss and said, "Okay let's go finish our snowman." So out the door they went. Jack began again making another giant snowball when suddenly, bang, Jack got hit with a snowball. Before Lynetta can make another one Jack got her back. Then there was a huge snowball fight then while Lynetta was making more Jack ran over, grabbed Lynetta and they rolled over in the snow. Jack tickled Lynetta till she hollered, "I give." So he stopped, held his hand out to help her up, then when she was back on her feet they kissed again. She asked, "Want some more hot cocoa?" "Sure. Let's go."

Looking at the half built snowman she said, "We didn't get very far on Mr. Snowman." "No we didn't but I had a lot of fun didn't you?" "Of course I did. I was with you. Shall we go inside?" "Yeah, let's go."

Inside, they got their hot cocoa but before they could sit down the phone rang. "Hello?" "Hi It's Dre." "Hi Dre, what's up?" "Oh, not much. You busy?" "Not right now. Jack and I just came in from a snowball fight. He won of course."- She laughed. "Oh Jack is there? I'll call back later." "No, we're just having some hot cocoa. Hey, why don't you come over and join us? Jack, is it okay with you if Adrianne comes over?" "Yeah, great. If she's here we might actually get our snowman made." "Did you hear that? Now you have to come over. We need you." "Okay I'll be right over. Bye now." "See ya." Jack said, "I have an idea. He grabbed his cell phone. (Lyn looked puzzled.)

Jack on the phone: "Hey what are you doing right now? Great. Get your winter gear on and come over to Lynetta's. Yes now!" He hung up and had a big smile on his face. "Alright who did you call?" "You'll see." he said with the smile still on his face.

Soon there was a knock at the door. Lynetta answered it. "Hi Dre. Come on in." Then a few minutes later, knock, knock, knock. Lynetta answered the door again. "Okay, I'm here. Where's the party? smile – Just kidding." Dre came over, "Hi Leon." "Hi Dre. I was hoping you'd be here." Lynetta gave Jack a look and he shrugged his shoulders with a little impish grin. Then Lynetta said, "Okay. Everyone, let's go outside."

All four of them went outside and began to finish Mr. Snowman. When they were nearly done Lynetta went inside to get the finishing touches. Soon she came back out as the guys were just putting his head on. Jack said, "There you go Mr. Snowman. You have your head on now." Dre said, "And we have the rest of him." They gave him 2 large button eyes, a carrot nose, 3 pieces of coal for a smile, a scarf for his neck and...something was missing. Jack said, "Wait a minute, just wait right there." He ran to his car opened the trunk and then came running back. "Here, check this out." He had a flat black circle, he hit the edge on his other arm and POP! Instant top hat. Lynetta said, "Cool, but where...?" "I found it at a second hand store." As he put it on their Snowman he said, "Well how does he look?" They all said, "Awesome." Finally Mr. Snowman was done. Lynetta said, "You know, with that top hat he almost looks alive." Jack said, "Yeah, he almost does." Lynetta said, "He's very handsome." "Hey wait a minute." "Oh, for a snowman. But he doesn't compare to you." "Okay, that's better." He smiled and kissed her.

Suddenly, bang. "Here we go again." Lynetta said. Then Jack replied, "Yeah but this time we have help." Soon all four were throwing snowballs at each other. Then it quickly turned into girls against the guys. All of a sudden someone yelled, "ATTACK!" The guys ran towards the girls with snowballs ready so the girls ran screaming the other way. But the guys were faster. They caught both girls and down they went into the snow. The guys said, "We have you now!" and with an evil laugh began to tickle them mercilessly. Jack stopped for a moment, looked at Lynetta and said, "Do you know how cute you look all covered in snow?" She said, "No." So he scooped up some snow and dumped it on her and said, "Adorable." "Oh you." Then he grabbed her and kissed her before she could get too mad.

Meanwhile, Leon and Adrianne were laying in the snow making snow angels. After Jack kissed Lynetta he said, "Oh baby, your lips are so cold. Leon, we should get them inside and warm them up." Leon took a glove off and touched Adrianne's face. "Wow, you're right. Dre are you cold?" "A little." Lyn said, "Let's all go in and I'll make us all some hot cocoa." Jack said, "Alright, I'm for that. Let's go." Leon said, "Oh, yeah."and Dre said, "I'll help you Lynetta." So they all went back inside.

A little later they were enjoying their hot cocoa. Lynetta went and stood by the front window and looked out at her snowman. Jack came up behind her and put his arm around her, "Looking at our snowman?" "Yeah." "Pretty cool don't you think?" He smiled. "Very funny. Actually I think he looks rather lonely. I was thinking, he should have a wife... and children." "Now wait a minute. First, remember how long it took to make *him*? And second, You don't have enough snow left to make him a wife." "Oh I know that. I was just thinking out loud. But it would be nice don't you think?" "Yes, I guess you're right."

"Hey sounds like someone put some music on. Shall we go dance?" "Sure." Jack and Lyn went back by the stereo where Leon and Adrianne were dancing, so Jack and Lyn joined in. Leon said, "I wondered if you two were going to come in and join us." After awhile Leon and Adrianne thanked Lynetta for a wonderful time and some great hot cocoa and they both left. Leon said to Dre, "Can I see you later?" "Sure. I'd like that." He smiled and kissed her cheek and they both got in their cars and left.

Later that afternoon Jack and Lynetta picked up her little sister Stella and took her sledding. After about an hour and a half Jack asked Stella, "Having fun or are you ready to head for home?" She replied, "Are you kidding? This is great! You both should try it. Jack you should have brought your snowboard. See, (she pointed to a small group, of beginning snowboarders.) You could go over and help them." Lynetta said, "Oh look, they're trying so hard. Jack, let's do that. Let's go help those kids learn how to snowboard." "I don't know. I'm not licensed or a pro snowboarder. I could get into trouble if someone got seriously hurt." "I know you're not either of those but neither are most big brothers. And you are really good at snowboarding." "Well I do okay." Stella burst in with "Would you two go on over there, you're cramping my style. she nodded and looked over at a cute boy. Lynetta looked at him then winked at Stella. "Come on Jack, she wants some space." "Okay let's go then."

Jack and Lynetta went over where there were about 6 or 7 beginning snowboarders to try and help them learn how to snowboard. About one hour later the kids began to head home with their parents. Each one of them thanked Jack and Lynetta for helping them. A few minutes later some parents came back and said to them, "Here I want to give you something for your time." and gave Jack and Lynetta some money. They both tried to refuse but the parents wouldn't take it back. Some asked if they would be there tomorrow and Jack said, "No, we only came to bring my girlfriend's little sister sledding." Soon all the junior snowboarders were gone and Jack and Lynetta went back to get Stella.

By then the sun was going down and it was getting colder. "Stella are you ready to go now?" "Y-y-y-yes. I'm tired and c-c-c-cold." Soon

Stella was back home and she asked, "Netta, will you and Jack stay and have some hot cocoa with me, pleeease?" They looked at each other, shrugged their shoulders then looked back at Stella, "Sure." Stella got the hot cocoa her mom had made and poured some for both of them, then for herself. After they were done she still wanted them to stay but mom said, "Stella, maybe they have other plans." "No, I'm sure they don't. You can stay can't you?" Jack smiled and said, "Okay sweetie, we'll stay, just for you." Stella was so happy.

They played games until Stella began to get sleepy and started to yawn. Then Jack said, "You know I have a great story I'll bet neither of you has ever heard. Want to hear it or shall I just keep it to myself?" Lynetta jumped in with, "Oh, I want to hear it. Please." And Stella said, "Me too – Me too." Then Jack said, I don't know. It's a pretty amazing story. Maybe I'd better keep it to myself." Then both girls pleaded with him, "PLEASE tell us, please, please!" "Okay, okay. Everybody get comfortable...", both girls cuddled up, one on each side of Jack and he began the story.

Once upon a time in a far away land there lived a young king who had no queen. In that same land in a village, not far from the young king, there lived a beautiful, fair haired maiden who had always dreamed of marrying a prince..." Jack continued his story until both young maidens at his side were fast asleep. Their mother came in and quietly said, "Now that is a picture I'll never forget. Here let me take Stella to bed." As she reached for Stella Jack suddenly said, "Oh please, let me do that. We can lay Lynetta over on the pillow while I carry Stella up to bed." "Oh how nice of you Jack. She is getting to weigh quite a bit." So her mom got a pillow and they laid Lynetta over on it. Then Jack got up and carefully picked up Stella and carried her on up to bed and covered her up. She began to wake up. "King Jack, thanks for the wonderful story. I love you." She fell back asleep and Jack said, "I love you too, princess Stella and he leaned over and kissed her forehead. Then he went downstairs and Lynetta was still asleep.

He said to Mrs. H., "Well I guess I should get this one home." But Mrs. H. put her hand on his arm and said, "Why don't you just let her sleep right there and I'll take her home in the morning." "Okay, if you say so." "Better yet, why don't you come over and I'll fix breakfast for everyone." "Are you sure?" "Oh yes, it will be wonderful." "Okay, it sounds terrific. What time?" "7:00?" "I'll be here." Jack kissed Lynetta goodnight and covered her with a blanket. He said, "Goodnight my Queen," then he went home.

Early next morning Jack was ready to go by 6:30. He had one stop to make before going over for breakfast. Mrs H. woke up Stella, "Almost time for breakfast, put your robe on and come on down I have a surprise for you." Stella got up and put her robe and slippers on wondering, "What surprise?"

Mrs. H. went downstairs to Lynetta, "Lynetta... Lyn..."there was a knock at the door. Mrs. H. left Lynetta and answered the door, "Yes? Oh, good morning Jack. I was just going to wake Lynetta. Stella should be right down." "Can I wake her, please?" "Sure, I'll get breakfast on the table." Before Mrs. H. turned to go to the kitchen Jack said, "Here, this is for you." He handed her a red rose. "What's this for?" "Special flowers for special ladies." "Thank you Jack. That was sweet of you. I'll get breakfast on now."

Jack went over to where Lynetta was still asleep and gave her a kiss. "Good morning sweetheart." He pushed her hair back from her face and kissed her again. "It's time to get up." She slowly opened her eyes. "What? What are *you* doing here? (she looked around) I fell asleep at my mom's?" "Yes. You must have been really tired. Both you and Stella fell asleep. I guess my little story did the trick a little too well." "I'm sorry Jack." "That's okay. I have something for you." He handed her a red rose. "Oh honey it's beautiful. Thank you." "You're welcome." She noticed his shirt. "Hey you weren't wearing that shirt yesterday, when did you change? And what happened last night?" Jack told her all about what happened after she fell asleep and why he was back this morning.

## "BREAKFAST!"

Mrs. H. was calling everyone to breakfast. Stella came bouncing down the stairs as usual. "Good morning mom. I had a wonderful dream last night. I'll tell you about it later. Now, what's the surprise?" Just then Jack and Lynetta came in from the other room. Stella blinked and shook her head. "Jack and Lynetta?" "Surprise. After Lynetta fell asleep and Jack put you to bed last night, for me, I invited him to have breakfast with us this morning." "Cool, mom." Jack went over to Stella with a big smile, "Good morning kiddo." Lynetta said, "Mom, I need a vase with some water in it, look what Jack brought me." She showed everyone her rose. "Well why don't you just put it in with mine on the table." "Oh wow! Jack you are just so sweet." Then Stella said, rather disappointed, "Wow, pretty flowers. I wish..." Just then with a huge smile Jack pulled the last rose from behind his back and handed it to Stella. "Now you didn't think I'd leave you out did you?" "Oh thank you so much." Stella reached up and Jack bent down so she could give him a great big hug and a kiss. Lynetta said, "Hey squirt." Jack said, "Well...?" and held his arms out to her. So Lynetta also gave him a hug and a BIG kiss. Mrs H. said, "Okay, enough kissing and hugging. Everyone please sit down and eat before it all gets cold. Everyone said, "YES MA'AM!"

After breakfast Jack thanked Mrs. H. for such a wonderful breakfast. And everyone pitched in to clear away the breakfast dishes. Jack said to Lynetta, "I should take you home so you can shower and change." "Thank you Jack." "I'm gonna take Lynetta home now. Thanks again. Goodbye." "Thanks for taking such good care of my daughter. Goodbye Jack. Come again. To Lynetta, "Goodbye honey."

"Goodbye mom, Squirt and thanks for everything. And breakfast was great."

Jack took Lynetta home. "I have some stuff to do, so I'll see you later, okay? I love you " "Same here. Thanks for the ride and...(she got up close to him-) thanks for last night. I just wish I hadn't fallen asleep." "But you looked so cute when you were sleeping." "By the way, I loved the story you were telling. You made it up didn't you?" "Guilty." "Will I see you later today?" "I hope so. But goodbye for now. This should hold you..." He gave her a long passionate kiss and left. Lynetta showered and changed and did a little house cleaning. Then she decided to go do a little shopping.

She went downtown and thought she'd check out some of the men's stores and sporting goods stores to find something special for Jack since he was so nice to Stella. Sporting goods just didn't have the right thing, so she tried the men's stores.

She didn't find anything in the first one. She went into the second one and began looking around. She looked across the store and there was Jack. She started over to say hi when all of a sudden she noticed a girl standing next to him and they appeared to be together. Then she thought, "That's crazy. He loves me. He would never..." She looked again and at that moment the couple turned toward each other and hugged. Then the girl threw her arms around the guy and kissed him.

He smiled at her and they turned to leave. Lynetta had to quickly duck out of sight. She didn't want Jack to see her.

She tried to follow them through the mall without them seeing her. She made it. Once outside, they went walking down the sidewalk and Lynetta watched them as they both got into Jack's car. The past five minutes played over and over in Lynetta's head as she went back to the mens store. She wandered around the store not really looking at anything specifically. Just then, a salesman came up and asked, "May I help you find something Miss?" She looked at him and started to cry. Then she said, "No Thank you. I won't be needing anything today." She hurried out of the store and went home in tears.

At home, Lynetta cried for quite awhile, then she just felt numb inside. She thought to herself, "How can he say he loves me and then turn around and cheat on me?" Her phone rang and she let the machine pick up. She heard the incoming call, "Hey it's Alyssa, call me when..." Lynetta answered the phone, "Hi, Alyssa?" "Oh, you are home. Is everything okay?" "Well, no." she started to cry again. "Oh, Lyn. Do you want me to come over?" "Would you please?" "Sure. I'll be right there."

They both hung up and in a few minutes Alyssa was knocking on Lyn's front door. "I'm here honey. What's wrong? Is it Jack? (she nodded) Is he hurt? (she shook her head) What? Tell me." Lynetta told Lyssa all about the shopping trip and then what she saw in the men's store between Jack and that girl. "Are you sure? Maybe you imagined it, or maybe it wasn't Jack." "But they got into his car." she said.

"Well maybe the car just looked like Jack's." "No. I know it was him. I had to duck out of sight as they walked right by me so he couldn't see me." "Oh Lynetta, I hope you're wrong. I just know he loves only you." "And what, he's just having a fling with her?" "I think you should go over and confront him, face to face. Let him know what you saw. Maybe there's a simple reason for what you saw." "There is. He's tired of me and wants someone new." "Do you love Jack?" "Yes." "Then you need to fight for your man." Her phone rang again. She let the machine pick up. Then she heard, "Hey baby it's me. Are you home? I want to come over and spend some more time with you or you could come over here. I love you baby! Call me." He hung up.

Lynetta was so confused. She was angry, hurt, sad and just plain didn't understand. Alyssa said, "Here's your chance. Call him back and talk to him." Lyn picked up the phone and started to dial but hung up again. "I-I can't. I…just can't do it." "Why not?" "What if he wants to date her? I'm not ready to hear that and I won't share him!" "Lynetta I don't know what else to tell you. Do you want to get out and go for a drive or something? Anything to get your mind off of this?" "No. Thanks. You can go if you want to." "Okay. I think you need some time alone. Call me if you need to talk, whatever time it is!" " Thanks Lyssa. You're a true friend. Goodnight." Then Lynetta called out, "And don't say any of this to anyone, *especially* Jack!"

"Okay." Sounding disappointed, "Darn." Lynetta didn't call Jack back so he called her again. "Lynetta? Are you home yet baby? I miss you so much. Where are you? Call me please, kiss, kiss." She couldn't stand hearing his voice like that so she tried again to pick up the phone but couldn't hold it. The receiver fell to the floor and Lynetta ran out the front door crying. She ran and ran until she couldn't run anymore. She found herself walking in a nearby park.

Jack got impatient and called again. "Busy, she must be home." He hung up so she could call him. But she didn't call. He kept trying, "Still busy. I know, Alyssa." He called Alyssa, "Hello?" "Lyssa it's Jack. Do you know if Lynetta is at home? I've been calling but I keep getting a busy signal." "Maybe she took the phone off the hook." "Thanks Lyssa." "Uh, Jack?" (then she remembered Lyn's warning: Don't tell Jack!) "Yes Lyssa?" "Uh, have a good night. Bye." Jack looked at the receiver and *suddenly* felt like something was very wrong. So he got in his car and quickly drove over to Lynetta's. He knocked but got no answer.

He called her mom, "Hello?" "Hi Stella? It's Jack. Is your sister there? I have to ask her something." "No. Sorry Jack. She isn't here. When are you coming over again? I miss you." "Soon Stella, right now I want to talk to Lynetta. See you soon, goodnight." Jack was really getting worried now. "Where are you babe? Adrianne's?"

"Hello?" "Dre, it's Jack is Lynetta with you?" She heard the worry in his voice. "No. Sorry Jack. We didn't even talk today. Is everything alright?" "I don't know. I can't find Lynetta anywhere. I've called everyone we know that she'd be with. No one knows where she is and I'm at her house. There's no answer at her door. I don't know what to think."

"Did you call Leon?" "No remember he's out of town on a shoot." "Oh yeah. Sorry Jack. Maybe she went for a drive?" "No, her car is still here." "Should we go tell her mom?" "No. Not till we know more." Adrianne looked out the window. "It's getting very dark Jack. We need to find her." "We need a search party. Are you in?" "You know it. I'll call Alyssa." "I'll call Brian and Jarrod. We'll meet at Lynetta's as soon as everyone can get here and HURRY." In minutes everyone was there with flashlights. "Okay, we'll split up into two groups. Dre, you and Brian are one team with a phone. Lyssa and Jarrod will go with me. Whoever sees her, call the other team immediately. Any questions? Let's go."

Lynetta was alone in the park and it was getting very dark. There was no moon or stars out tonight. Her mind started seeing things and she started to hear strange noises. Everything looked so different at night. She didn't recognize anything and her cell phone was nearly dead. She had one bar showing and it was flashing. She called Lyssa, "You have reached my voice mail, please leave a message after the tone." " I'll try Dre." ring "Hello?" "Dre?" "Who-" "*static*" "Lynetta? Lynetta is that you? Where are you?" "static- help- static- nothing"

Dre called Jack. "Talk to me." "Lynetta just called me. She sounded like she's in trouble but then her phone went dead." "Let's check the park. If her phone was nearly dead she has to be close by or her signal wouldn't get through." They went to the park, decided where she might have gone and headed out.

Lynetta heard someone calling to her, "Hey baby, going my way?" She didn't know the voice so she kept going, walking faster and trying to ignore the guys behind her. "Are you lost? I can help." The voice was right behind her now and her blood ran cold. She was sure this was the end. Just then... she heard Adrianne's voice calling, "Lynetta!" Lynetta screamed, "Help me please, I'm over here. Help me, help me!" The guys heard several voices. When they turned around and saw all the lights coming towards them they took off. In seconds, Dre reached Lynetta and they gave each other a great big hug. "Are you okay Lynetta?" "I am now, thanks to you." Dre called Jack, "I have her, we're by the swings, she's a little shaken but she's okay. What happened?" "I guess I got turned around in the dark and I got lost. Thank you so much." "It wasn't just me. You should really thank the one who organized the search party." "Search party? What? Who?" Dre said, "Who? Who else?" Lynetta heard a familiar deep voice say, "Thank God and all the angels you're alright. I don't know what I'd do if anything ever happened to you." "Jack." "Come here baby."

He wrapped his arms around her and gave her a huge hug. Suddenly her anger came flooding back and she broke free of his embrace. Jack didn't understand why she pulled away so abruptly. So he said to her, "Baby, it's me. I'm here. Everything is okay now. Let's get you home." She thanked everyone else for coming to help find her, everyone that is, but Jack. She didn't say a word all the way home. Everybody said how glad they all were that she was alright and went home. Everyone but Alyssa. Alyssa thought she ought to stick around to keep the fireworks under control.

Once inside Jack could tell something was bothering Lynetta but he didn't know what. So he asked, "What's wrong?" Lynetta didn't quite know how to answer him. Then Alyssa said, "Do you want me to ask him?" "No." "Ask me what?" Jack was really confused now. Lynetta took a deep breath and said, "Okay. Just tell me who you're in love with?" He looked even more puzzled and said, "You of course." "And how many girls are you seeing other than me?" "None. (he turned to Alyssa) What's she talking about Lyssa?" Lynetta continued, "Jack, were you in a men's store earlier today?" "Yeah, but how did you know?" "So, who was the cute little blond I saw you with?" He thought back to the store. "Oh, you mean Sue?" Lynetta looked surprised. So did Alyssa. Lyn said, "You admit it?"

"What? Wait..., wait a minute, you think that Sue, and I, me. Hold on. Sue is Dylan's new girlfriend. She wanted to get something special for their 1 week anniversary and she wanted me to help since I know Dylan's tastes better than she does. So when she said what she wanted to buy I took her down to Dylan's favorite men's store, G.Q. and showed her some things Dylan's had his eye on for awhile. After she decided on something and bought it, she was so excited she said to me, 'He'll love it', threw her arms around me in a big bear hug and then she kissed me. I was so surprised. I was smiling because I knew my brother had finally found a very special girl just like I have. And I was hoping that she makes him as happy as you make me."

"Oh Jack. I'm sorry. I was so wrong. Can you forgive me?" "Sure, I love you, remember?" Lyssa said to herself, "I thought as much." Then she said, "Goodnight you two. I'm going home." Jack said, "Goodnight Alyssa and thanks." "Yeah Lyssa thanks for helping them find me. Goodnight."

Jack looked at Lynetta and said, in a very serious tone, "Are you absolutely, positively, <u>sure</u> you're alright?" "Yes Jack. I am just fine." "I'm so sorry. It just hit me. It's my fault you were out there. If anything had happened to you I'd never forgive myself." "It's okay Jack, I'm here. I'm fine. Will you stop? It's all over now and we're here together. Now look at me. (he looked into her face) I'm just as much to blame. I should have had more faith and trust in you. I should have come to you right away and told you what I saw. Instead, I doubted you and jumped to wrong conclusions."

"And I should have told you that I was taking Dylan's girlfriend shopping. But I never thought you'd see us in a men's store. By the way, what were *you* doing in a men's store anyway?" "Me? I-I-well, I-uh..." "Never mind. I'm sure I'll find out." She smiled. Jack said, "It's late. I should go and let you get some sleep." "Well I <u>am</u> kind of tired. So I think I will go to bed. Goodnight Jack. I love you." "Goodnight babe and sweet dreams. I love you too." They kissed once more and Jack went home.

# *Twelve*

## *The Night of the Masquerade Ball*

It was late November and winter was almost here. People were beginning to make plans for holiday parties. Fall Festivals, Come-as-you-are parties, Costume parties and every kind of Christmas party one could think of. But there has always been *one* that, to me, will always stand out above all the rest. And that will always be, the one and *only* "Masquerade Ball". Complete with beautiful, elaborate masks and costumes and ladies in their beautiful ball gowns and the men in their tuxedos.

Lynetta said, "It would be so much fun to go to a Masquerade Ball." Adrianne said, "Oh yeah and you could win a prize for most original costume." Alyssa said, "Yeah and think of all the different kinds of food and drinks that are offered." The guys were thinking about the music and dancing at all the parties, so they can dance with their girls.

Friday night the girls got together at Alyssa's for a sleepover. The same night the guys all went over to Jarrod's just to hang out for awhile.

One by one the girls showed up at Alyssa's. Soon everyone was there and they were all talking about the holidays coming up. Lynetta said, "I really wish someone we knew would have a Masquerade Ball this year. That would be so cool." Dre said, "Yeah I know and I have the best idea for a costume." Alyssa said, "Hey why don't we have one of our own? We can invite whoever we want to." Lynetta said, "Yeah and we can make it so all our younger brothers and sisters can come, like my sister Stella and Jack's brother Dylan." Dre said, "Let's do it. We could have it 2 weeks before Christmas so anyone going away for the Christmas holidays can still come."

Lynetta said, "My mom would love to help with the decorating and baking some of the goodies." Adrianne said, "My mom could help with the punch and other drinks, she has some great party punch recipes." Alyssa said, I could get my mom to print up some colorful posters, banners and invitations. I can't wait to get started. But it will have to wait at least until tomorrow." Lyn said, "Yeah it is rather late." Dre said, "I'm turning in. See you in the morning. Goodnight." The girls all said goodnight and turned in.

At Jarrod's the guys found a football game on T.V. and were watching the final minutes of the game. Bang, it's over. "Well guys you can crash here if you want, I'm turning in and it looks like Leon's asleep already. Goodnight. See you tomorrow."

The next morning the girls woke up and were all excited about their upcoming plans. Alyssa said, "Lynetta, do you think Jack will want to help out?" "I don't really know. I could ask him." "Great, let me know as soon as possible." Adrianne said, "Leon might help with the music and the D.J."

Lyssa began thinking out loud, "First we need a big enough place to hold a lot of people, then we need tables, chairs, etc..." Then Dre said to Lynetta, "I think Alyssa needs a secretary." "No kidding. Hey Lyssa?" She stopped for a moment, "Huh?" She looked over at Dre and, "Oh, sorry. When it comes to having a party I get carried away sometimes."

Just then the phone rang. Lyssa picked up, "Hello?" "Hello gorgeous." "Oh Hi Jarrod." "How's my girl this morning?" "Fine, how are you?" "I miss you but I'll be okay. What are you girls doing?" (in the background, "Ask her already"), "Nothing, just talking, why?" "Well, we wanted to know if you girls would like to go to breakfast with us?"

"H mm, I don't know let me ask, Hey, does anybody here want to have breakfast with the boys?" They all gathered around the phone and shouted into the phone, "YES!"

Jarrod quickly pulled the phone away from his ear, then he said, "Whoa." Alyssa said, "Sorry baby, I guess that was a bit loud." "Shall we pick you girls up or meet you there?" "Where are you going?" "The Waffle Place." "Sounds great. Why don't we meet you there. About half an hour?" "Okay half an hour. See you then, bye darlin'." "Bye Jarrod."

Half an hour later the girls arrived for breakfast. The guys were waiting for them in the lobby and when the girls came in they all went in and had breakfast together. Jarrod asked Alyssa, "So, what do you girls have planned for today?" "Funny you happened to put it that way." "What do you mean?" "Well, we were talking about having a Masquerade ball, 2 weeks before Christmas, with costumes, decorations, food and drinks and no alcohol so our younger brothers and sisters can come. What do you think?" "Sounds great. Can I help?" Jack, Leon and Brian all said, "Yeah, count us in." "Thanks guys, we were hoping you'd want to help. There's plenty to do."

Everyone was helping with the plans for the big party. Things were really starting to take shape and the girls were getting all excited. A friend of Alyssa's heard about it and wanted to help. "Are you going to sell tickets?" "No Katie. It's by invitation." "Oh, well I could make a list of names and check them off..." "Katie it won't be that formal. If anybody that has a costume and a mask wants to join us they can. It's called an open invitation." "Okay."

Alyssa found a dance hall available for the night they wanted it and reserved it. The decorations and all the food was ready for the green light. Two days before, the moms were busy in their kitchens preparing all the food. The day before, everyone was busy decorating the dance hall. The only thing they were allowed to do was put up wall decorations and streamers.

Suddenly Alyssa got a call from the manager of the dance hall. "Hello? This is Alyssa." "Hello Miss Tillman. This is Mr. Schubert, the manager of the dance hall you reserved." "Oh, Hi, what can I do for you? Is there a problem with the hall? We can still use it can't we?" She was beginning to panic. "Calm down, calm down everything is fine, I just called to tell you the class that was going to use the hall tomorrow just called to cancel so if you want to set up a little earlier than you planned I won't charge you for the extra time." "I don't understand."

"I can't refund the other party's money because they canceled too late and I can't rent it this late so I thought you could use the extra time. You could say it was rented for you." "So we can go on in early and get it all ready?" "That is correct." "Oh, thank you." she said excitedly. "You're welcome. And have a wonderful time."

"Mr. Schubert?" "Call me Tom, please." "Tom, why don't you stop by and have a glass of punch and bring your lady. We'd love to have you." "Well thank you Miss Tillman. I just might do that." "Alyssa, please Tom." "Alyssa, until the ball. Goodbye." "Goodbye Tom."

"Lynetta, you'll never guess what just happened." "So tell me." "The dance hall manager just called me and said we can start setting up tomorrow morning because the class that was going to be there just canceled and get this, he won't charge us because they canceled too late to get their money back. Isn't that cool?" "Great. So we can bring in the chairs and tables tomorrow morning to set up?" "Yes." Jack came over when he heard Alyssa so excited. "Hey, what's up?" "Alyssa just got some super news. We can start setting up tomorrow morning." "Alright. I'll go tell the guys."

Everyone came over at 9 a. m. sharp and started setting up. Alyssa's cousin, Katie, was in town and came along to help. In a couple of hours they finished decorating. Everyone stood back and took a good look at what they had done. Alyssa said, "Now all we need is the food, drinks and..." Adrianne said, "PEOPLE!" she smiled. Lynetta said, "Lyssa you've done a great job." She replied, "What do you mean me? WE did a great job. Thank you everyone. This only happened because of all of you."

"Yeah but Lyssa you organized it all. That's a huge part of it. And you kept us all going when some of us wanted to quit." Dre said, Lynetta's right Lyssa and you know it." "Well thanks but I had a great crew behind me. So, thanks again everyone." Katie looked over at Jack and said, "Oh, he's cute." Alyssa heard her and said, "Who is?" "The guy with the long, brown hair and the incredible blue eyes." "Yeah and he's taken." "By who?" "Lynetta. So don't even try. He only has eyes for her." "What, are they married?" "No. But all you have to do is look at them to see the sparks between them." "Oh whatever." Katie saw a challenge she just couldn't ignore.

She went over to Lynetta and said, "Hey, can I ask you something?" "Sure." "I was wondering what you're wearing for a costume tonight? I can't think of anything." "Okay, I'll tell you but don't tell Jack. I want to surprise him and see if he can guess it's me." "Oh I get it. That's so cool." "Yeah I thought so." "Well do you know what he's wearing?" "Not yet. But I will soon." Lynetta told Katie all about her costume.

Alyssa was busy getting everyone's attention. "Okay everyone, it looks great and it's only 3 p.m. So lets all go home and get ready for tonight. I want to see everyone here at 5:30. See you later." Everyone told Alyssa bye and see you later as they all headed for home.

Katie went over where Jack and Leon were talking. She overheard part of their conversation. "So Jack what's your costume going to be?" Jack and Leon told each other what they're going to wear but Katie couldn't quite hear. "Oh snap, they're too quiet. I have to find out what he's wearing tonight." Alyssa got everyone to leave so she could lock up.

Lynetta said to Katie, "Wanna come to my house? We can find or make a costume for you." "Okay, if you're sure." "Oh definitely." So Katie went to Lynetta's house. After searching awhile they couldn't find the costume Lyn was thinking of. Then all of a sudden, "Wait, I know where it is! It's in my mom's attic. I'll give her a call and see if she can find it."

Meanwhile, Lyn showed Kattie her costume. "Wow, that's beautiful." "Isn't it?" Lynetta's mom called back. "Lynetta, I found it and it's in great shape. Shall I bring it over?" "No we'll come and get it. Thanks bye." The girls jumped into Lyn's car and went to her mom's house. Lynetta introduced Katie to her mom and her sister Stella. "Hi nice to meet you, Katie?" "Yes ma'am. Nice to meet you." "Well I think this dress will be perfect on you." "Thank you so much Mrs. H." "You're very welcome. I'm glad I could find it." "Katie do you just want to get ready at my house?" "Well sure, it would save time." "Okay then. Let's go." So they took the dress back to Lyn's house. Back at Lynetta's house Lyn said, "Let's get ready for the party." "Okay, where?" "You can use the bathroom in my room and I'll use the other one. I'll just leave my costume in the bedroom till I'm all ready. See you soon. Oh, you can put some music on if you want to." "Thanks."

Katie went and put the stereo on and then went in to get ready. She thought to herself, "This is turning out better than I planned."

Katie finished getting ready and put Lynetta's costume on instead of hers. Then she quietly walked over to the bathroom where Lynetta was getting ready and after she found a chair, wedged it tightly, under the doorknob. Then she went over to the stereo and turned the volume up so no one could hear Lynetta if she began to yell for help. Katie took Lynetta's keys and whispered, "Thanks Lynetta for everything. And I mean <u>everything</u>."

Katie turned and saw a picture of Jack on the table. She went over to it and as she picked it up she said, "You'll be mine tonight, baby." Then she kissed his face and left. She got into Lyn's car and went to the ball. She made sure no one saw *her* drive up in Lynetta's car. She parked quickly and before she got out of the car, she put her mask on. Then she practiced imitating Lynetta's voice and gestures. In her best Lynetta voice, "Well here I go."

She went to the door and went on in. "I'd better avoid her mom and sister as much as I can. They might give me away."

Stella was just putting her mask on. The mothers were getting the rest of the food and drinks on, as well as cups, plates, etc. "I'd better go volunteer to help. I'm sure Lynetta would. She's such a goody two shoes, bah." Katie went over to the table and imitating Lynetta's voice asked, "Can I help?" Mrs. H. said, "Sure honey, would you set a few cups out and put ice in them please?" "Sure- of course. Half full right?" "That's good. Would one of you boys go get the punchbowl and put it here on the table please?" "I will Mrs. H." "Thank you Jack. I mean, young man, whoever you are." She smiled at him. Katie said under her breath, "So that's Jack. Okay." It was ten minutes before seven and everything was ready for their guests.

Meanwhile, back at Lyn's house, Lynetta had discovered she was trapped in the bathroom. She pounded on the door and yelled, "Katie the door is stuck can you help me?" Then she noticed the stereo was turned up louder than before, so she yelled louder. But Katie didn't answer. She tried turning the door knob and pulling as hard as she could, nothing. Then after a bit she tried the door knob again and realized it's really stuck. So she called again, "Katie the door is stuck can you help me, please? KATIE. Where is she?"

Back at the ball Katie had discovered which one Jack was, so she walked over to him, "Hi having a good time?" "Uh, yeah so far. You?" "So far." "The place looks awesome and all the food smells so good."

"Yeah, mom, I mean Mrs. H. really out did herself." He smiled at her. "No one's dancing yet, shall we start it off?" "Okay." Just then the music changed to a fast song. Katie was thinking, "Oh no I hope I can dance like her." Then Jack said, "Oh man I wanted a slow one. Not fair. Oh well, there's always the next one, right?" "Yeah, right." She thought, "Whew! That was close!" (Dre was beginning to wonder by now where Katie was, since she was supposed to be checking coats in.) She went over to Mrs. H., "Excuse me but do you know if Katie is here? She's supposed to be our coat check girl." "No Adrianne, I don't. But Lynetta is dancing with uh..., someone." She smiled. Mrs. H. pointed her out. "Oh, thanks." "Sure. Did you get something to eat dear?" "Uh maybe later."

Dre went over to the couple Mrs. H. pointed out. "Hi guys. Do either of you know where Katie is? She's supposed to be the coat check girl." Jack said, "No, sorry Dre we haven't seen her, have we?", (Katie shook her head). "But didn't she come with you?" "I took her home earlier so she could bring her car." Dre gave a funny look to "Lyn" and said, "I think you need something to drink. Your voice sounds a bit hoarse. Want me to get you something?" "No. I'm fine. Really." she replied. "Okay, (she looked at both of them) is everything alright with you two?" Jack said, "Yeah, why do you ask?" "Oh, nothing, I just hope Katie is alright. Bye." Dre walked away with a strange feeling, turned to look at the pair again and shook her head.

Back at Lynetta's house: Lynetta was still trapped in the bathroom. She finally started looking through the drawers to find anything that might get her out of there. Then in one drawer she saw a metal nail file. She remembered watching a movie where someone used one to pry the hinge pins loose so she decided to give it a try. "This isn't as easy as they made it look but I have to get out of here." Finally the first one came out. She carefully worked each one out then pulled on the door knob. It gave a little but wouldn't open, like something was holding it. She shoved it with her shoulder. It gave a little more. She kept doing it hoping she'd be able to move whatever was holding or blocking the door.

Back at the ball: Dre went to Alyssa, "Lyssa, where is your cousin Katie? She's an hour and a half late." "Sorry Dre. I don't know." "Can you call her?" "No I don't have her cell number and her new phone is being hooked up tomorrow morning." "She should have called if she was going to be late. Especially this late. She knew we'd be counting on her." "I'm sorry Dre. I'll be the coat check girl till she gets here." "No! You organized everything. You need to be able to float around and check on things. I'll do the coats." "Are you sure?" "Yes. I'm sure. By the way have you noticed anything strange about Jack and Lynetta tonight? I talked to them earlier and I got some really strange vibes coming from them." "I haven't talked to them but now that you mention it I wonder if they had a fight or a disagreement of some kind?" "I don't know it just seems weird. I'll see you later, oh, and by the way, great party Lyssa. Bye." "Thanks, see ya."

Finally the D.J. put on a slow song and Katie started to walk away but Jack grabbed her arm and pulled her back. "Oh no! We're not missing another slow one. I want to hold my baby in my arms and dance with her. Okay?" They went out on the floor and Jack put his arms around Katie and they cuddled and danced. Katie thought: "At last I'm in your arms and you're holding *me*!"

Once again, back at Lynetta's house, she almost had the door open. "Okay this is it. The moment of truth." She backed up as far as she could and ran full force at the hinged side of the door and finally it opened. "A chair against the door, great. Well at least I'm out of there." She turned and looked once more at the bathroom. Then Lynetta went into the bedroom and saw Katie's costume on the bed. "So that's her little game. You better not be up to what I think you are." Lynetta put on Katie's costume. She couldn't find her keys, so she went outside only to find her car was gone. "Katie."

Lynetta was going to call Jack or one of her friends at the ball but Katie had managed to disable both of Lyn's phones so she went to the neighbors. "Hi, I'm sorry to bother you, my phone isn't working. May I borrow your phone to call a taxi please?" "Sure Lynetta, do you need a ride somewhere dear? I can take you anywhere you need to go. Going to a costume party?" "Yes and I'm very late." "Say no more. Let's go." "Are you sure?" "You're one of the nicest neighbors I have. It's the least I could do for you. (at the car) Get in." "Thank you so much. I'll pay you back. I promise." "No you won't! This is my chance to pay *you* back for all your kindness and your boyfriend's too." "I don't do so much." "Don't argue with me young lady. Anyway, you can't win this one, so just accept it dear." Lynetta smiled "Okay Mrs. B.,you win and thank you." "Thank you. Ah here we are. Have a good time dear." "Mrs.

B. Would you like to come in? We have tons of food and drinks and there's no alcohol." "Oh, no dear it's almost my bedtime, but thank you all the same. Goodnight." "Goodnight Mrs. B. and thanks again for the ride." "You're welcome, give Jack a hug for me." Lynetta gave her a hug before she left, then she went inside posing as Katie.

Jack and Katie were dancing to another slow song. Every time Jack had tried to kiss her before she had turned away or walked away but this time he was determined. He looked into her eyes and gently lifted her chin up to kiss her. At the same time Lynetta, dressed as Katie, walked in. She went to the food table and said, "Hi mommy." Then she turned to her sister and said, "Hi squirt." Both of them together said, "Lynetta? But, then who...?"

Just then Lynetta saw Jack and Katie about to kiss, but inches from her lips, Jack said, "This is as close as you'll ever get." Katie had a shocked look on her face, then he let go of her and walked away. He started to leave then he felt a familiar touch on his arm. As he turned around to see who it was, another girl in costume said, "Don't go yet. It's early. Stay, with me, please?"

He looked at her and said, "Only if you pass the test." "What test?" "My test. First question. "Who do I mean when I say L.?" "Lynetta." "Okay, #2. True or False? Lynetta *likes* to be called Netta?" "FALSE, I hate that name, except when Stella calls me that." "#3. What do you call your mom?" "Mommy or Mama." "Alright, #4. Who is Stella?" "My, I mean Lynetta's younger sister." "#5. By what nickname does Lynetta call Stella?" "Squirt, what else?" "Okay, and #6. What is my favorite color?" "Let me see..., you like blue and green and...brown, actually you don't have a favorite because you like all colors. So, do I pass?" Jack walked up to her, looked into her eyes, took her in his arms and said, "Not, Yet, dance with me." "But there's no music." "If you are who I think you are, we don't need any music. So dance with me." "Okay, let's go."

He lead her to the dance floor and slipped his arms around her as she laid her head on his shoulder. They danced as if the music was already playing, then he lifted her chin up to face him and passionately kissed her. "How did you know it was me?" "Because, you're the only one who makes me feel this way even if I can't see your face. We have a chemistry no one can fake. I love you baby " "And I love you Jack." She took her mask off and everyone in the room gasped.

Dre said, "I thought something wasn't right. So this must be... (Adrianne took Katie's mask off), I thought so. Well Katie what do you have to say now?" She looked at Jack and said, "But you almost kissed me, not Lynetta, ME. Why didn't you?" "I just wanted to see how far you'd really go." "You mean you knew I wasn't Lynetta?" "Not at first, but I've known Lynetta a long time and when you're in love with someone you can't be fooled by imitations." Katie looked at Lynetta, "Okay, now what are you going to do to me?"

Alyssa and Lynetta made Katie check coats the rest of the night, like she was supposed to. Then she had to put all empty plates, cups and used napkins into the trash. After that, she went and took all the trash out. By then it was 11:00 p. m. and <u>finally</u> they let her sit down.

Just as she sat down a young man came over to ask her to dance. "Hello, would you like to dance?" "Okay, sure." She got up to dance but she was so tired she said, "I don't suppose you'd want to sit this one out with me would you? We could just sit and talk." "Sure, I'm not a very good dancer, anyway."

They went over and sat down together. He said, "By the way my name is Paul." "I'm Katie." They talked awhile and were really enjoying each other's company when Alyssa came over and asked Paul, "Would you like to dance?" He asked Katie, "Would you mind?" Before she could answer Alyssa said, Katie? No, she won't mind a bit."

Alyssa grabbed Paul's hand and they hit the dance floor for a few songs. Suddenly Jarrod tapped Paul's shoulder and asked, "May I cut in?" Paul stepped aside, said, "Thank you" to Alyssa and went back to Katie. Jarrod said, What's with you and Paul?" "Oh nothing. I just wanted to give Katie a taste of what Lynetta felt when she saw Katie dancing with Jack earlier." " I wish you had told me your plan. I was starting to get a little jealous." "Really?" "Yes, you're <u>my</u> girl. Don't forget that." "I won't. Not as long as you're around to remind me." "Then I'll tell you <u>every</u> day." Then he kissed her.

Jack and Lynetta were dancing but Lynetta had a question on her mind ever since she got to the ball. Jack noticed something was bothering Lynetta so he asked, "Okay, what's wrong? Something is bothering you, tell me." "I'm not sure. In my head I keep seeing you almost kiss Katie and I was wondering would you have kissed her anyway if I hadn't shown up?"

"Is that what's bothering you?" "Yes! Well would you have?" "No,

I *knew* she wasn't you. I guess the best way to explain it is when you're even *near* me I can feel your presence and I didn't feel *anything* with her even dancing with her. But I didn't know where you were until you walked into the room and *instantly* I knew you were here, <u>somewhere</u>. So I let her think I was going to kiss her till the last moment when I let her know it wasn't going to happen." "I love you Jack." "I love you too baby. Do you feel better now?" "Yes." "Dance with me some more?" "I'd love to." So Jack and Lynetta went out to the middle of the floor and danced the night away.

After the food and drinks were almost gone and almost everyone had gone home Jack said to Lynetta, "May I take you home?" And she replied, "Of course you may kind sir." So Jack took Lynetta home. At her door he said, "Always remember, I Love YOU!" Then he kissed her goodnight and she said, "I love you too Jack, always!"

## THE END